W9-CBP-651

WILDER BOYS

THE JOURNEY HOME

SEE HOW THE JOURNEY BEGAN

Wilder Boys

WILDER BOYS

THE JOURNEY HOME

BRANDON WALLACE

ALADDIN

NEW YORK   LONDON   TORONTO   SYDNEY   NEW DELHI

This book is a work of fiction. Any references to historical events, real people, or real places are used fictitiously. Other names, characters, places, and events are products of the author's imagination, and any resemblance to actual events or places or persons, living or dead, is entirely coincidental.

ALADDIN
An imprint of Simon & Schuster Children's Publishing Division
1230 Avenue of the Americas, New York, New York 10020
First Aladdin hardcover edition January 2016
Text copyright © 2016 by Hothouse Fiction
Jacket illustration copyright © 2016 by Thomas Flintham
All rights reserved, including the right of reproduction
in whole or in part in any form.
ALADDIN is a trademark of Simon & Schuster, Inc., and related logo
is a registered trademark of Simon & Schuster, Inc.
For information about special discounts for bulk purchases,
please contact Simon & Schuster Special Sales at 1-866-506-1949
or business@simonandschuster.com.
The Simon & Schuster Speakers Bureau can bring authors to your live event.
For more information or to book an event, contact the Simon & Schuster Speakers Bureau
at 1-866-248-3049 or visit our website at www.simonspeakers.com.
Jacket designed by Karin Paprocki
Interior designed by Mike Rosamilia
Interior illustrations by Jon Howard
The text of this book was set in Alright Sans.
Manufactured in the United States of America 1120 FFG
2 4 6 8 10 9 7 5 3
Library of Congress Cataloging-in-Publication Data
Wallace, Brandon, author.
The journey home / by Brandon Wallace.—Hardcover edition.
pages cm.—(Wilder boys ; [2])
Summary: When Jake, thirteen, and Taylor, eleven, learn that their mother is still alive
but facing grave danger if they do not return the money they took from her abusive
boyfriend, Bull, they leave their father, who is not eager to help, and set off on their own
again for a late autumn trek from Wyoming to Pittsburgh.
[1. Survival—Fiction. 2. Wilderness areas—Fiction. 3. Brothers—Fiction.
4. Runaways—Fiction. 5. Voyages and travels—Fiction.
6. Family problems—Fiction.] I. Title.
PZ7.1.W35Jou 2016
[Fic]—dc23
2015016108
ISBN 978-1-4814-3267-2 (hc)
ISBN 978-1-4814-3268-9 (eBook)

To Jordan Yager and all other great Riverton readers!
And a special thanks to Sneed B. Collard III.

WILDER BOYS

THE JOURNEY HOME

1

Jake Wilder moved through the dense forest, making as little noise as he could. His breath steamed in the shafts of afternoon light slanting down through the trees. The chill in the air was like the hunger in his stomach; gnawing, but bearable. Just about.

A thought flashed through his mind: *I used to be able to pick up a burger and fries for a few bucks.*

He closed his eyes. Images of golden fries and neon-red ketchup surfaced in his memory, and the knot of hunger tightened. Sometimes it hurt to have left all that behind.

Get a grip, he told himself. *Focus on the hunt.*

He flicked his eyes open again and took a breath.

The beauty of the forest all around him was unlike anything he had seen back home in Pennsylvania. This high in the Tetons, the aspen leaves had already begun to shift from summer green to autumn gold. But the birdsong that had brought the forest to life over the summer had disappeared; almost all the birds had flown south. The forest had a haunted, silent feel now, like an abandoned house.

There was still life here, though, if you knew where to look for it. Jake paused and dropped down to squat on his haunches, looking at the fresh rabbit droppings that littered the forest floor. There were still plenty of rabbits for the taking. The trick, of course, was knowing *how*. . . .

Jake made his way to the spot he'd picked out several days before, the entrance to a burrow near the edge of the forest. The two pegs he'd driven into the ground were still there.

Working quickly, he fitted a small cross branch into two sockets cut into the pegs. Dangling from the cross branch was a loop of cord tied with a slipknot that would tighten around an animal's neck.

Now for the trap, Jake thought. He pulled his dark hair back out of his eyes and bent a nearby sapling down toward the ground. He tied the cross branch to it with a piece of string. The crossbar strained with tension but didn't slip loose from its sockets. But if anything nudged it—like a rabbit—it would pop free and whip upward with lethal force.

Satisfied, Jake crept back through the foliage and sat down on a log.

"And now," he whispered to himself, "we wait."

Jake picked at a scab on his hand and let his thoughts wander back to his old life. He and his younger brother, Taylor, had lived a normal-enough life back in Pittsburgh. That was, until his mom's brutal boyfriend, Bull, had beaten her and threatened them. Convinced that their mother was dead, they knew they had to get away, to a place where Bull couldn't reach them. So they'd taken Bull's money and struck out for Wyoming, in the crazy hope of finding the father they barely remembered.

But Bull had followed them, desperate to get his money back and to silence the boys permanently. He'd chased them across half the country, all the way up into the mountains, where their dad, Abe, was living. Jake shivered as he remembered the day when Abe had fought like a grizzly to protect the boys. If their dad hadn't shown up when he had, the boys would have been dead meat. Instead, it was Bull who had died, plunging over a mountain waterfall. Jake tried to feel sorry for the man, but it was difficult after everything that had happened.

A flicker of movement in the corner of his eye snapped Jake back to reality. He quickly turned his head and trained his sight on the burrow to see the furry brown head of a mountain cottontail emerge. Even from a distance Jake could see the rabbit's ears twitch, trying to sense danger. Jake continued to breathe slowly and steadily, not moving an inch.

The rabbit seemed to think it was safe. It came all the way out of the burrow. It again sniffed the air and studied the forest in all directions.

Jake held his breath.

Come on, Mr. Rabbit . . . keep going.

As Jake watched, the rabbit hopped along the path. Jake could feel his muscles tense as the animal's head got caught in the snare's loop and pulled the cross branch free of the pegs.

Zing!

The sapling sprang instantly upward, jerking the rabbit into the air by its neck.

Heart thundering, Jake leaped to his feet and raced forward.

"Got you!" he cried.

Adrenaline washed through him. The rabbit was hanging, limp, not struggling—a clean kill.

He undid the noose and excitedly took his catch. He peered into the rabbit's dead eyes, which only moments ago had gleamed as they'd looked around for danger.

Before uncertainty could creep through him, he reassured himself. *I'm only doing it to survive.* Out here Jake could see the truth of what "killing to live" really meant, and he never took an animal's life for granted. He carefully placed the rabbit in his pack and broke down the trap, and then set off back toward his dad's cabin, pride washing through him.

BRANDON WALLACE

As he emerged from the forest into a small clearing, Jake found his dad and brother sitting around the fire pit outside the cabin. Warm flames crackled in the pit, and the smell of campfire smoke filled the air.

"Hey, buddy! There you are."

Abe sat in the shadow of a simple wooden dwelling, tending the campfire. Taylor sat in a growing patch of white shavings, busy whittling on a branch with a hunting knife.

"Hey, Dad!" Jake called back.

He hadn't known what to expect when they'd first arrived in the wilderness. He'd thought maybe they'd be making their clothes from skins and hunting or foraging for all their food. But although Abe lived off the land as much as possible, he wasn't a hermit; he was a park ranger. He was allowed to live in his little cabin as part of his job—keeping an eye out for forest fires, monitoring wildlife, and keeping trails clear.

The boys' Jack Russell terrier, Cody, raced over to greet Jake.

"Hey, boy!" Jake squatted down and affectionately tussled with the dog, letting Cody wriggle and squirm through his arms.

"You okay?" Abe asked. "You were gone awhile."

"Wanted to work on my trapping skills."

Abe nodded, his weather-beaten face wrinkling with good humor. "Good idea."

Taylor paused in his whittling, his green eyes flashing anxiously up at Jake. "How'd it go?"

Jake straightened up and stepped over to the fire, warming his hands above the flames. Then, unable to suppress a smile, he opened his pack and pulled out the dead rabbit.

Cody raised his nose in the air, circling Jake, trying to catch the rabbit's scent.

Taylor looked stunned for a second, and then a smile spread across his face. "Way to go!" he cried.

"Thanks, Bro!" Jake laughed, pulling the rabbit away from the eager dog.

Abe grinned at Jake. "Looks like all that hard work paid off."

"Thanks, Dad," Jake said, and grinned. He looked into the flames. Being back with their dad after so many years was great—he'd taught them so much since they'd been here. Not just the normal school subjects but all about the wilderness, which he knew like the back of his hand.

Taylor caught the look on Jake's face and laughed. "You do know we'll need more than one rabbit to get through the winter, right?"

"Of course I know that!" Jake snapped back. *Way to ruin the moment, Taylor.*

"Leave him alone, Taylor," Abe said. "Winter's nothing to joke about. My first winter in this place nearly killed me."

That explains a lot, Jake thought. Their dad was

preparing for winter as if he were readying a castle for a coming siege. In fact, the thought of winter was beginning to scare Jake.

Abe seemed to sense Jake's discomfort. He reached for his guitar and plucked a few long, melancholy notes that reminded Jake of wolves howling in the distance. "Did I ever tell you boys about that first winter?"

Jake and Taylor shook their heads.

"Well then, listen up."

Taylor hunkered down beside his dad to listen, wrapping Cody under one arm. Jake sat on a stump and warmed his hands by the fire. On the horizon the sun was setting and the dark was already drawing in.

"I'd been out hunting all day long. Just me, all alone in the cold, with a sack of dead rabbits," he began. "It got dark real quick, and I should have headed for home right away, but I got greedy. I had one more rabbit in my sights, a big, fat one. He was pure white, like the spirit of winter."

"Did you catch him?" Taylor asked.

"'Fraid not, buddy. He got away, but not before he'd led me deep into the woods. I was totally lost." Abe plucked a *whap-whap-waaa* sad set of chords that made the boys laugh.

"It seems funny now," he continued, "but back then I was scared to death. Especially when I figured out I wasn't alone. There were eyes watching between the trees. Hungry eyes."

"Wolves?" Taylor gasped.

"A whole pack of them," Abe said, his eyes flashing. "The leader was a gray, one-eyed brute. They wanted the rabbits I was bringing home. And I knew that once they were done eating them, they'd start on me."

Jake leaned forward, listening hard.

"But then I found it: Polaris, the North Star," their dad continued, pointing up at the darkening sky. "Right there at the tip of the Little Dipper's handle."

"Then what?" Jake asked. Out of the corner of his eye he saw Taylor stand up and rummage around in his pocket. Jake was about to ask what Taylor was up to, when his dad fixed him tight with his stare.

"That star guided me right out of those woods. I was bruised and shook up, but thankfully I'd managed to lose the wolves. Once I figured out which way was north, I headed up to the hills to build a snow house and . . ."

As Abe went on talking, Taylor crept up behind him and pulled out the wooden carving he'd been working on earlier.

"Raargh!" he yelled, waving the carving in his dad's face. It was a miniature wolf with gaping jaws.

"Argh!" Abe cried, caught off guard. He let a broad grin arc across his bearded face. "You nearly had me!" He dropped his guitar and wrestled Taylor and his wolf to the ground.

Jake just laughed. "You didn't escape those wolves after all. . . ."

"This one's much fiercer than a wolf," Abe said, and chuckled, letting go of Taylor.

"It's coming for you next, Jake," Taylor growled, brandishing the carving in his brother's face.

Jake added another log to the campfire and sat back, in mock fright.

"You know, Jake," Abe said, turning back to winter. "That rabbit of yours couldn't have come at a better time."

"What do you mean?" Taylor asked.

Abe poured him a mug of hot broth from his flask. "Thanksgiving's just a few weeks away, and the snows could come any day now. We need to eat well tonight, because tomorrow we're heading into town for the last of our supplies."

Jake laughed. "Supplies? I thought we had everything we needed right here."

Abe patted him on the shoulder. "There're *some* needs nature can't provide. Unfortunately, we can't tap a tree for kerosene, or dig up knife blades. Wyoming winters can be harsh. You know how long we might get snowed in for up here?"

Jake thought it over. "Six weeks?" he said, fearing the worst. It would be tough, but he figured they could survive being cut off from the world for that long.

"Sorry, Jake," Abe sighed, his brows knitting together. "It's more like six months."

2

Winter announced itself the next day with a wind that howled around the cabin, stealing down the smoke hole, feathering the water in the sink with ice, and creeping under blankets to gnaw on the boys' toes.

Outside, Abe looked at the horizon with troubled eyes, but Jake and Taylor laughed as they set off across the rugged terrain. Five months ago neither of the boys could have imagined making the journey to town in a single day, but their time with Abe and the cross-country trek to find him had toughened them up. Even heavy backpacks wouldn't slow them down.

Cody trotted along ahead of them, sniffing trees and cocking his leg here and there as if he owned the wilderness. Abe pointed out the natural features of the landscape around them, carefully explaining the signs of animal and plant life. Taylor drank it all in, but Jake tuned it out. He was thinking about the town they were heading for, where he could eat hot food he hadn't had to cook, and stock up on books. Six months without even a magazine to read would drive him crazy.

"Now, this one's really useful," Abe suddenly announced, pointing to a plant with some shriveled brown leaves and taller flower stalks rising from the center.

Taylor looked closely at the plant, his brow knitted in concentration. Then his face brightened. "I know this one! It's the weapons plant."

Abe looked at him quizzically.

"You know, *arrow*leaf balsamroot?"

"Oh yeah, you're right," Abe said. "You can use it to treat burns and other wounds, and it makes a pretty good cough medicine too."

"Like when Jake healed my leg . . . ," Taylor said.

Abe cocked his head.

"Remember, right before we found you, Taylor got attacked by a bobcat," Jake explained.

Abe nodded. "Of course I remember, and you were real smart about what to do."

Jake remembered how often Bull had called him stupid, or worse. He relished the sound of his father's encouragement.

Abe handed out a midmorning snack of pemmican—a

mixture of crushed elk meat, fat, and berries—as they continued onward.

"Hey, Jake," Taylor said with his mouth full, "can you imagine what the kids at school would say if they knew we were out here? Or Mr. Polanachek?"

Jake laughed, thinking about their grouchy school bus driver back in Pittsburgh. "He'd have a cow."

"I know, right." Taylor turned to look up at Jake. "In a weird way I kind of miss going to school. I mean, homeschooling is fun and all, but I miss being around our friends."

Before Jake could answer, Abe cut in. "You might miss school, but you don't miss the city, do you? It's so much healthier out here. No pollution, no crime, no junk food."

"I guess you really hated the city when you lived there, huh?" Taylor asked. He fell into step with his father.

Jake hung back, listening.

Abe thought about that. "The way I see it, I never lived in the city. Nobody can *live* in a city! All you can do is waste away, slowly, a day at a time."

"Sounds like a line from one of your songs," Jake cut in.

Abe coughed. "Guilty as charged."

Jake laughed, but his father's attitude still rankled. Not for the first time, it annoyed him how Abe saw everything in stark black-and-white. Sure, the mountains were beautiful and pure. But there were lots of good things about cities, too, like libraries, parks, and restaurants. Not to mention friends. He knew there was no point arguing about it, though. Abe always thought his way of thinking was right.

If life is so perfect out here, Dad, why didn't you ever come to get us yourself? Why didn't you bring me, Taylor, and Mom out here with you?

Jake tried to push his frustration out of his mind and just enjoy the time they had with their father now.

A few yards later Taylor stepped off the trail and darted into the undergrowth. "Back in a sec," he called.

"What's he up to?" Jake laughed as he watched Taylor dash to the edge of the forest and rummage around on the ground. When he straightened up, Taylor held a medium-size white-capped mushroom in his hand.

"Who's hungry?" Taylor said with a laugh.

Abe leaped forward and knocked the mushroom from Taylor's hands.

"Never eat that one!" he said, alarm cracking his voice. "Didn't I tell you never to eat something you aren't sure of?"

Taylor looked shaken. "But, Dad, I wasn't going to . . ."

Abe held him tight for a moment, then released his grip. "Taylor, that's a Deadly Parasol! One bite, just one, and you'd have been dead."

Jake stepped in. "Dad, it's okay. Taylor wasn't going to eat it. He was just showing it to us."

Abe looked from one boy to the other. Then he took a deep breath, bent down, and hiked up the leg of his jeans.

Both the boys saw the ugly white mass of scar tissue on his left calf.

"See that?"

They nodded.

"That's what happened last time I got careless out in the wild."

"Is it a snake bite?" Jake guessed.

Abe didn't answer. He just rolled his pants leg back down. "You can never let your guard down out here." He sighed deeply. "Let's get a move on."

Jake thought back to his dad ranting about how bad the city was. But snake bites and deadly mushrooms? It wasn't as perfect here as his dad made it out to be.

When they reached town two hours later, Jake felt a huge wave of relief to be back in civilization. There were only a few dozen houses, a post office, a gas station, and a general store that doubled as an information center for visitors, but after being away from other people for so long, even a tiny roadside stop felt like a bustling metropolis to Jake.

Abe left Cody sitting outside and shepherded the boys into the general store that fronted the two-lane highway. The boys looked around like starving wolves.

"Look at all this stuff, Jake!" Taylor exclaimed.

The store offered everything a person could want: groceries, guns and ammo, camping supplies, propane and kerosene, tools and hardware. Jake imagined how much easier life would be if their cabin had one of the shiny propane grills the store had for sale.

Abe briskly shook hands with the manager, Gunter, who wore over his long blond hair a baseball-style hat from a group called the Rocky Mountain Elk Foundation. He turned to the boys and flashed them a hearty smile. "You two look like you're going to be even taller than your dad here."

The boys glanced at each other sheepishly. It was true that they'd grown since leaving Pennsylvania. With their long hair and tanned faces, they were turning into mini-Abes.

"So, Abe, you here to stock up for winter?" Gunter asked, leaning on the counter.

Abe whipped out a list and handed it to the storekeeper. "It's about that time, Gunter."

Gunter scanned the list, nodding. "This won't take but a few minutes."

"The quicker the better," Abe said. "So we can get home before dark."

"I could have gotten it ready in advance if you'd called ahead—"

"Called ahead? Dad doesn't have a *phone*," Taylor interrupted.

Gunter raised an eyebrow, and eventually Abe spoke up. "Well . . . I do, actually. For work emergencies. Forest fires, lost ramblers, that kind of thing."

If there was a phone in the cabin, what other technology did Abe have squirreled away, Jake suddenly wondered.

"You sell any books?" Jake asked, looking around eagerly.

Gunter scratched the side of his face. "Not really. . . . I have a few magazines in back. You might find something there."

"Thanks."

Jake headed to the rear of the store while Taylor made a beeline for the candy shelves. Jake found a rack of magazines, mostly sports stuff that interested him about as much as wet cardboard. *Great. Just great.* Six months with only *Sports Illustrated* to read.

"You all right back there?" Abe called.

"Coming!" he cried. Before he left the aisle, a stack of small, hardback notebooks on a shelf caught his eye. Over the past few months he'd wanted to start keeping a diary of his and Taylor's adventures—kind of like the wilderness journal Abe had kept when he'd been younger. It was Abe's old journal that had inspired the boys to make the trip to Wyoming, and had helped them survive the journey. Jake grabbed a notebook and went to get Taylor, who was still drooling over the snacks section.

"Think dad will get us one?" Taylor asked, sweeping his hand through his sandy brown hair.

"Doesn't have to be his call, does it?" said Jake, picking up a bag of peanut butter cups.

"What do you mean?" Taylor asked, confused.

"Nothing. . . . C'mon," he said.

On the counter, Gunter had stacked a treasure pile of supplies: boxes of nails, duct tape, gun oil, gun cartridges, a new ax, shoelaces, matches, sewing needles and thread . . .

"We'll take these, too," Jake said, placing the notebook and peanut butter cups down.

Abe picked up the bag of candy and dangled it as if it were a dead rat. "This crap?"

"The candy's for me," Taylor quickly said, sensing his dad's disapproval. "It's okay. I'll put it back."

"C'mon, Abe. It won't kill 'em," Gunter said.

"Yeah," Jake chipped in. "It's hardly a deadly mushroom."

Abe's eyebrow arched, and for a moment it looked like he was going to launch into one of his long speeches, but he dropped the candy back onto the counter.

"You're right. But I get a bite!" he said with a laugh, handing over the money.

3

As the three of them headed toward the front of the store, laden with goods, the door opened before they could reach it. Suddenly the mood changed again. Jake's squabble with his dad was forgotten, and tension took over.

A police officer stood in the doorway, arms folded, eyes narrowed.

Jake froze.

One thought went screaming through his mind: *Bull. They've found his body.* He exchanged glances with Taylor and saw the fear in his eyes.

He wished they'd worked out a story to tell the police before they'd come to town. But no, that would have meant *talking* about Bull's death, and that was the one thing they never, ever did.

"That your dog out front?" the cop asked.

"Yeah, he's ours," Jake said. His throat felt dry and tight. "Is he okay?"

"He's loose!" snapped the policeman. "If you're going to visit a national park, you'd better learn the rules. Dogs must be kept under control at all times."

Abe finally spoke up. "It's my fault, Officer. I thought he was tied up."

The policeman frowned. "Abe Wilder, isn't it?"

"That's right."

"Well, I know *you* know the rules." He looked sternly at Jake and Taylor. "Just checking that these boys know them too." The police officer turned to leave, but then paused. "Oh, Mr. Wilder? One more thing . . ."

Abe swallowed. "Yes?"

"You should bring that guitar of yours next time you come by. Play a few songs over at Benny's. It's been too long."

Abe smiled, and promised he would.

They said their good-byes and made to start the trek home.

"C'mon," Abe muttered distractedly. "Let's get out of here."

Jake couldn't help notice the change that had come over his dad—jaw set, sweat beading on his forehead, eyes darting nervously.

Once again the memory of Bull's last scream rang

out in Jake's mind. He saw the limp body collapse over the waterfall's edge and go tumbling down. It was as if Bull's ghost were haunting them.

On the day before Thanksgiving, Jake and Taylor stirred a blackened iron pot hanging over the fire pit outside the cabin. Since their trip into town, the weather had grown colder, and now the two boys huddled close to the open flames. Puffs of fog escaped from their mouths as they breathed.

"You think it's ready?" Taylor asked, peering into the pot.

"How would I know? I've never boiled balsamroot before."

"Feels more like Halloween than Thanksgiving, huh?" Taylor grinned and stirred some more. "Abracadabra!"

Jake laughed. "Don't want to burn yourself before the medicine is done."

Abe had given Jake and Taylor the job of digging up, cleaning, cutting, and shredding the arrowleaf balsamroot before dropping it into a pot of slow-boiling water. They'd been hard at work all morning.

"Y'know, they had Band-Aids and antiseptic back at the store," Jake said drily. It was as if their dad were trying to cram them full of wilderness knowledge to get back all those years when he hadn't been around.

"Yeah, but this is way cooler," Taylor said. Nothing could dampen his spirits.

The cabin door banged open, and Abe appeared. "How's that medicine coming?"

"We think it's almost done," said Taylor.

"Looks good. Take it off to cool and then get the rifles."

Taylor's eyes widened, and Jake sat bolt upright. "Are we going hunting?"

"Tomorrow's Thanksgiving," Abe answered. "So we need to get ourselves some dinner."

A half hour later Abe, the boys, and Cody were following a game trail along a stream that ran down from the higher mountain peaks. Despite the cold, Jake's palms were sweaty where they gripped his rifle.

Usually Abe carried the main rifle, a .30-06, but today he went empty-handed. "I'm leaving the shooting to you two today," he'd said. "You guys are going to bring home Thanksgiving dinner."

"No pressure, then," Jake had said, grinning. Abe had smiled back.

Back at home in Pennsylvania a gun had been a thing of fear, but out here the weight of it felt almost reassuring in his hands. It was strange how something so dangerous now felt useful. Instead of using guns to intimidate people, like Bull had done, they were using them for survival.

As they walked, Cody flushed out a small flock of turkeys. Jake jumped at the sudden flurry of wings and instantly cursed himself for being so on edge. Taylor, with a cooler head, leveled his gun and took aim.

"No!" Abe yelled. "Don't shoot!"

"Huh?" Taylor blinked.

"Better to have a shotgun for those, buddy. Besides, we don't want to scare off any larger game."

Reluctantly Taylor lowered the rifle.

It wasn't long before Jake spotted signs of the "larger game" his dad was after. He held up his hand, and they all froze. "Prints!" he whispered. "See there, along the stream? They're split. That means deer."

Cody began sniffing excitedly, while Abe, Jake, and Taylor squatted down to examine the tracks.

"White-tailed?" Taylor asked.

"Probably mulies," said Abe. "They're a bit bigger. The tracks look fresh too. Want to try to catch up with them?"

"What do you think?" Jake replied with a chuckle.

They set off at a faster pace. There were no jokes now. Nobody said a word. They communicated in gestures and glances.

After they'd followed the trail through the trees, the tracks suddenly split into two separate groups.

"Now what?" Taylor whispered, breaking the silence.

"We split up," Abe said under his breath. "Taylor, come with me. We'll go after the larger group. Jake, you and Cody follow the other tracks."

Jake gave a curt nod. They'd make less noise separately,

and it might increase their chances of getting a shot at something.

Abe drew them into a close huddle and whispered, "If one of us gets a deer, fire an extra shot to alert the others to come help out. A single shot means a miss or smaller game, so keep hunting. If none of us bags anything, meet up back at the cabin by sunset."

Jake knew that wasn't going to happen—there was no way he was going back empty-handed.

While Abe and Taylor followed the stream, Jake and Cody set out after the smaller group of deer. From the number of tracks, Jake guessed they were from two, maybe three animals at most. He placed his feet carefully, avoiding dried branches or leaves that might make noise and alert the deer that they were being pursued.

As he walked up a steep slope dotted with pines, Jake could feel his heart pounding like a jackhammer. The only living things he'd shot in his life so far were a couple of rats, and though he'd practiced in the little range their dad had set up, he was way below Taylor's standard. Being sent out on his own, with only Cody for company, felt like a test.

Doubt surged up in his mind. *What if I just injure the deer and it runs away? What if I miss and scare away the group Dad and Taylor are following? What if we have root stew for Thanksgiving dinner because I can't shoot straight? Am I really cut out for all this?*

The triumph of snaring the rabbit seemed like a distant memory. Catching a rabbit in a trap was one thing. Shooting an animal bigger than himself was something else entirely.

Jake cursed himself when he lost the trail over some rocky ground, but to his relief, Cody had his nose firmly locked on to the deer's scent. They entered a thicket of aspen trees where the newly fallen leaves carpeted the ground in gold. It felt like entering a temple. Jake paused for a second, feeling the stillness all around.

Cody gave a little impatient whine.

Okay, okay, I'm coming.

As he and Cody moved deeper into the grove, the fallen leaves muffling their footsteps, Jake's senses were on high alert.

Stay calm, Jake. Don't blow it.

He and Cody slowly picked their way around the white aspen trunks, stepping over fallen branches. As they approached the far side of the thicket, Cody suddenly stopped.

Jake froze.

Three mule deer stood before him, all of them young bucks. At first Jake couldn't make out what they were doing, but then he saw one deer rise up onto its back legs to nibble the tip of an aspen branch. The other two bucks were munching shoots coming up from the ground.

Fattening up for the winter, Jake thought. *Sorry, guys, but we need to eat too. . . .*

Busy feeding, the deer hadn't noticed Jake and Cody approach, and Jake planned to keep it that way. He carefully removed a shell from his vest pocket and quietly chambered it into the rifle.

Now all he needed was the best firing position he could find. He stepped gingerly to a nearby aspen trunk that was tilting over at an angle. As Cody looked on, nose quivering, Jake rested the rifle barrel against the aspen trunk and took aim.

Ghost-white tree trunks partially blocked two of the mulies, but the third one foraged in full view. As Jake tried to steady the rifle, he could hear his blood thundering in his ears. Adrenaline made his hands shake, and the image of the deer bounced and quivered.

Suddenly, unwanted images came crowding into his head. His mom on the ambulance gurney. Bull screaming as he fell over the edge to his death.

Come on. Concentrate. He shook the thoughts out of his mind and took a deep breath. Planting his feet firmly at shoulder width, he rested the butt of the rifle against his shoulder and aimed at a spot right behind the deer's front shoulder.

Remembering what he'd been taught, Jake focused on his breathing, steady and deep. Without once taking his eye off his target, Jake flicked off the rifle's safety and eased his right forefinger onto the trigger.

Suddenly the deer raised his head and looked straight in Jake's direction.

Jake quickly squeezed and pulled the trigger. . . .

4

The sharp crack of the rifle split the mountain air. Quickly lowering his gun, Jake caught the movement of the two other bucks bounding into some nearby brush. There was no sign of the deer he'd targeted.

"C'mon, Cody!" Jake shouted, shouldering the rifle. "Let's go!"

The terrier sprinted ahead. Jake hurried after him, worried the deer might have escaped. Worse, he could have botched the shot and injured it, condemning it to a slow and painful death.

When he reached the spot where the deer had been standing, he saw the animal lying still, eyes glazed. Bright red blood trickled from its mouth and a quarter-size hole behind the shoulder.

I got it! Jake thought, fighting the urge to whoop.

Jake knelt and ran his hand over the still-warm body, while Cody sniffed the deer's face and neck. The buck's pelt felt smooth and soft under Jake's fingers.

"I did it," he whispered to himself. "Oh, man."

Just like he had when he'd snared the rabbit, he felt pride mixed with a touch of regret. He wondered if he'd ever stop feeling that way, but decided he never wanted to. He would never be someone who could kill a living creature without sadness.

His dad had to see this, though, right now. Jake stood, slipped another cartridge into the rifle, and pointed the gun into the air. A second shot would announce his triumph and bring Abe and Taylor running.

But before he could pull the trigger, Jake heard a branch crack behind him. They were here already.

"You've got to see this . . . ," he began, but his voice trailed off as Cody began barking furiously. Then Jake heard a snarl that chilled his blood.

He spun around. Slowly advancing on him, its jaws hanging open, was a lean, gray animal. A wolf? No—a coyote. And by the look of it, it wanted his kill too.

Jake's blood ran cold. "Get lost," he called. "Go!"

The coyote seemed to grin at him, as if to say *I don't think so*, and continued to pad toward him.

From behind Jake heard more twigs cracking. He

glanced over his shoulder and saw a second coyote, padding stealthily in his direction.

Cody dashed back and forth, barking fit to burst. Jake prayed the noise was enough to alert his dad and Taylor. One coyote was bad enough, but two meant he was outnumbered. For all he knew, there were even more of them out there, hiding between the trees.

He had to get out of there.

The first coyote bared its teeth and lunged. Jake snapped out of his trance. He lowered the rifle to fire, but the coyote was moving too fast. Brushing past Cody, it snapped at Jake's leg, sending him staggering backward.

Jake turned and ran as fast as he could. He sprinted through the trees, not looking back, until he neared the edge of the stream. With no other way across, he got ready to jump.

His foot skidded in the wet mud. Suddenly he was falling, arms flailing, into the freezing flood of the stream. "Argh!" he gasped, and struggled to pull himself upright, dripping and half-blind. He saw the coyote coming for him. In the distance he heard Cody's shrill whining.

They got Cody!

Jake stumbled to his feet, his soaked pants clinging to his legs, and fumbled for the rifle. Rage filled him. Any creature that hurt his dog was going to die.

Suddenly the big coyote was on him again, snapping

and snarling. Jake kicked, trying to shake the animal off, and the rifle flew out of his hands. A vicious tug at his leg sent him toppling over backward. His skull whacked against a stone.

Pain shot through his head and made him cry out. Dizzy and sick, he fought for his life against snapping jaws. Teeth tore at his jacket as he felt himself fading in and out of consciousness.

A gunshot rang through the trees. *Did I do that?* Jake thought deliriously.

A second shot sounded, and the coyote let go of him. He heard the scrabbling of claws as the animal fled.

And then everything went dark.

"Jake! Jake, are you okay?" Taylor yelled.

Jake sat up, wincing. A fresh bolt of pain broke across his head, and he sank back down with a groan. The trees above him were going in and out of focus.

His dad's shape loomed over him. "Jake?"

"Huh?" Jake mumbled.

Then Jake remembered the anguished whining. "Is Cody all right?"

Jake felt his dad wrap something around him. Then strong arms lifted him to his feet. He walked as best he could, drifting in and out of reality, tripping over rocks and tree roots. He caught glimpses of the forest and sky, and vaguely heard his father and brother talking, but it was like he was walking through a dream—a nightmare he couldn't wake up from.

Jake opened his eyes to find himself in bed. A Clark's nut-cracker called from somewhere outside.

"Taylor?" he mumbled.

"Jake!"

Taylor had been rocking back and forth in Abe's rocking chair but now instantly hurried over to the bed. Cody beat him to it. The terrier hopped up next to Jake and began licking his cheek and ears.

"Easy, boy," Jake moaned.

"Jake, are you okay?" Taylor asked, perching on the edge of the bed. "How do you feel?"

"I feel like someone used me for a piñata." He blinked sore eyes. "Is it dark yet?"

Taylor laughed. "Jake, it's *morning*. You slept the whole night."

Jake could feel that something was wrong with his leg. He pulled back the quilt. His ankle had been bound tight with a soft leather wrap.

"Don't you remember? A coyote bit you. Me and Dad cleaned it up and made a wrap with the balsamroot medicine. Dad scared the coyotes away," Taylor told him. "And Cody helped."

"Thanks, buddy," Jake said, scratching Cody around the neck and ears. "I owe you one."

"Dad's butchering your deer out front," Taylor said. "You remember the deer, right?"

Jake nodded.

Taylor gently punched him in the shoulder. "Awesome shot, Jake."

"Ouch." Jake rubbed his shoulder.

"Sorry. Want some more aspirin?"

"Yeah. And water."

While Taylor went to fetch them, Jake closed his eyes and tried to relax. He couldn't. His ankle throbbed. Weren't you meant to get a shot from a doctor when a wild animal bit you? All he had was an arrowleaf balsamroot poultice. Medicine he'd boiled up himself.

"What are we *doing* out here?" he whispered to himself.

I could have died. Those coyotes could have torn my throat out. If Taylor and Dad hadn't gotten there right then . . .

"Here you go." Taylor was back, with a cup of water and the aspirin. Jake swallowed them down.

"Taylor," he asked, handing the cup back to his brother, "do you ever wonder if we did the right thing coming here?"

Taylor looked confused. "What do you mean?"

Jake chose his words carefully. "I mean, it's great to be with Dad again, and it's cool to live somewhere so beautiful, but . . ."

"But what?"

Jake sighed. "I mean, this life is crazy. Look at everything we've had to deal with. The bobcat, running out of water, and now coyotes? How long before something really bad happens and we can't get to a hospital because we're out here in the middle of nowhere?"

"Dad knows what he's doing. He'll keep us safe."

Jake sank back down, feeling worse than ever. When he'd first come here, he'd felt free. For the first time in his life, he could run anywhere he wanted—there were no fences, no rules. Now those summer days were gone, the winter was drawing in, and he felt like a prisoner.

"We're going to be stuck here all winter," he said.

"Well, *I* like it here," said Taylor. "Dad's fun."

"What about Mom?" Jake asked softly. "What do you think she'd say if she knew we were living like this?"

The corners of Taylor's mouth sagged.

Jake squeezed his brother's shoulder.

"We didn't even get to say good-bye . . ." Taylor said.

Then his lips pressed together, and his eyes shifted away. At first Jake thought he was crying. But he wasn't. It was Taylor's scheming face.

"What is it?"

Taylor's eyes met his. "I know we can't bring Mom back," he said, "but . . ."

"What?"

"I found something that might help."

"Spit it out already," Jake said.

"Remember in the store, when Dad said he had a phone?

Well, while I was digging through the first aid chest for the aspirin, I found it."

Jake sat up straighter. "Seriously?"

"*Seriously.*" Taylor hurried to the first aid chest. Moments later he lifted out a large handset and brought it over to Jake. Cody sniffed at it and backed away, unimpressed.

"Geez," Jake said, feeling the weight of the phone, "it looks like one of those giant cell phones you see in old movies."

"I thought if Mom's answering machine is still turned on, we could, y'know, listen to her voice one more time."

"Let's try it," Jake said instantly. He had to do this quickly before he changed his mind. He took a deep breath and flipped the on switch above the number pad. A spluttering red light flicked into life.

Heart racing, Jake punched in the numbers he knew by heart. The earpiece popped and clicked like a broken-down radio.

"Sorry, Taylor. I don't think it's going to go through."

More clicks. Then he heard another sound. A ringing.

"It's ringing!" Jake said, and pressed the phone to his ear.

Taylor lifted Cody out of the way and huddled in as close as he could.

Heads together, they listened to the line ring. Jake knew what he'd hear next. *The number you are calling is not in service. Please hang up and dial again.*

The ringing tone stopped. Silence. And then:

"Hi, this is Jennifer Wilder. I'm not home right now . . ."

Jake and Taylor sat like rabbits in headlights, unable to breathe, listening to their mom's voice. For some reason the old answering machine was still working. Jake silently thanked whatever power had made that happen.

"It's like she's alive," Taylor whispered.

Jake's throat tightened. They listened to the entire message, all the way to the beep.

Taylor mouthed the words, *Should we say something?*

Jake shook his head.

There's no point. Mom's gone, Jake thought.

Just as Jake was about to hang up, however, he heard faint words coming from the earpiece.

"Wait. I'm here," the voice said. "Don't hang up."

Jake quickly raised the phone back to his ear, his heart galloping wildly.

"Hello?" he asked cautiously.

"Hello?" came the other voice again. "Who is this?"

"MOM?" Jake and Taylor shouted together.

"Jake! Taylor! Is that you?"

The phone crackled, but there was no doubt who the voice on the other end belonged to.

"Mom! It's us!" Jake shouted. "You're alive!"

5

"Oh my God!" Jennifer cried on the other end. "Are you okay?"

"We're fine!" Jake burst out. "Mom, you're okay. I can't believe it!"

"Of course I am, honey! I've been worried *sick*. When I woke up in the hospital and you weren't there . . ."

Jake thought back a few months to when Bull had put their mom in the hospital. They'd known they had to get out of there.

"Where are you boys?"

Breathe, Jake told himself. He forced himself to calm down. "We're in Wyoming with Dad."

"You're WHAT? Jake, did you just say 'Wyoming'?"

"YES! We came out here, and . . . Mom, we're sorry we left. We had to."

"Bull said you were dead!" Taylor howled. "We never should've believed him!"

There was silence for a second. Then their mom asked, "Have you heard from Bull?"

"No," Jake said quickly. "We don't know where he is. He could be anywhere."

"Jake, please!" There was worry in Jennifer's voice, but she sounded more determined than Jake had heard for years. "If you know anything about where he is, don't be afraid to tell me."

"Mom, I'm telling the truth. We haven't heard from him. We don't know anything."

The boys heard static, then the words "Bull . . . missing . . . money?"

Jake felt a fresh wave of panic. The ancient phone was cutting out.

"What, Mom? What did you say?" Jake pleaded. "I can't hear you!"

"Bull's friends keep asking where he is," their mom said, her voice frantic. "Well, not exactly friends. I think I'm in a lot of trouble. . . ."

"You don't have to worry about Bull anymore!" Taylor shouted happily, drowning out their mom's words. Jake managed not to shove him off the bed, but only just. He made a throat-cutting gesture at Taylor. Taylor nodded, wide-eyed, his mouth clamped shut.

"What do you mean, Mom?" Jake almost shouted. "What kind of trouble?"

There was a long pause, and Jake worried that the line had cut out. But then he heard a terrified whisper:

"Bull's boss says he's going to shoot me!"

Jake reeled back, as if hit by a bolt of lightning. He knew what he had to do, and the words were out before he had a chance to stop them.

"We're coming, Mom."

"No!" Jennifer yelled. "Stay with your dad! You can't come. It's too—"

And right then the connection died.

Jake looked at the phone. The red power light was dark. Frantically he pressed the power button, but it was no use.

Jake and Taylor stared at each other for a second. Then they rushed outside to find their dad.

Jake forgot all about his injured ankle. He could have been walking on air.

"Dad!" Taylor shouted. "It's Mom! She's okay. She's home!"

"What?" Abe asked, as if he couldn't believe what he was hearing. "What do you mean?"

"Mom," Jake said. "She's alive. And she's home! She's okay!"

Abe froze. "Boys, that's not funny. There are some things you just don't joke about."

"No joke," said Taylor. "We just talked to her on your phone. We wanted to hear her voice," Taylor continued. "So we called our old number and got the message machine. And then she picked up!"

Abe put down the tools he was using to work on the deer. "You're sure?" he asked incredulously. "One hundred percent sure it was her?"

"Positive," Jake said. "The connection was bad, and then the battery went dead, but not before we got to talk."

Abe looked from Taylor to Jake. A stunned smile crept across his face. His eyes lit up like Jake had never seen. "And what did she say? Is she okay?"

"We told her we were here with you and that we were fine. But, Dad, she said she's in a lot of trouble," Jake said.

Taylor blurted out, "Bull's boss is going to kill her!"

Abe suddenly darkened. "Slow down. Tell me exactly what she said."

Jake filled his dad in on the whole conversation and watched as he went through a lifetime of emotions—happy that Jennifer was okay, but disturbed at the dark turn her life had taken.

"I can't believe it," Abe muttered, unable to take it all in, pulling Jake and Taylor into a protective hug. "I know you must be worried, boys. I am too. But the most important thing is that she's alive. It looks like this Thanksgiving we've got a lot to be thankful for."

6 The rest of the afternoon the boys helped prepare a feast while Abe finished butchering the deer. The main course would be roast venison with wild onions, carrots, and potatoes, along with steamed wild asparagus they'd harvested earlier in the season. For dessert, wild berry cobbler cooked in a Dutch oven.

Jake hadn't cooked anything fancy at home in Pittsburgh, so he couldn't wait to show his mom how much he'd learned. He glanced at the table and thought, *We'll need another chair soon.* He grinned. Soon Mom would be here with them, safe from harm.

Taylor was still bubbling over from the phone call. "Don't you think Mom's going to love it out here?" he asked

Jake, for what must have been the eighteenth time that hour. "We'll be a family again!"

Jake hacked an onion in half. "We need to keep her safe. That's all that matters."

Taylor nodded, thinking it over. "The guys looking for Bull must be the ones who hired him to do the job he messed up."

"Probably," Jake said, remembering the horrible fight they'd witnessed several months ago. Bull had fought with a man who had come to get back money . . . there was a shot . . . Jake and Taylor had taken the money when they'd fled to Wyoming.

"Dad will know what to do. If we set off tomorrow, we can get Mom back here before the snows come," Taylor said.

Abe crashed in through the door, his arms full of firewood. A blast of icy air followed him in. He turned around and kicked the door shut, then dumped the wood down by the stove.

"Dad," Taylor asked, "what are we going to do? Can we leave tomorrow to go and get Mom?"

Abe said nothing, but Jake saw that his eyes were red and weary. He smacked the dirt off his hands. He avoided looking either of the boys in the eye.

"Smells good in here," he said quietly. "There's nothing quite like fresh meat you've seen to yourself. Jake, set the table, please."

Jake did as he was told, but the tension set him on edge. It reminded him of being back in Pittsburgh—the meals eaten in silence, the fearful glances at Bull, the dread of an argument waiting to erupt.

"Dad?" Taylor insisted. "When are we leaving to get Mom?"

"You don't understand, boys," Abe said, shuffling awkwardly from one foot to the other. Eventually he looked up and finally met their eyes. "We're not."

Jake and Taylor sat deathly still. Finally Taylor asked, "You mean we're not going tomorrow? But we'll go soon, right?"

"I mean we're not going at all," Abe said, in a sad voice just above a whisper.

Without another word Abe went outside, leaving Jake and Taylor to stare at each other, stunned. Then, at the same time, they scooted their chairs back and raced after him. They found Abe next to the outdoor fire pit, staring at the dying embers.

"Dad," Jake asked, "what are you talking about? We can't leave Mom in Pittsburgh. Didn't you hear us? She's in danger!"

"She needs our help, Dad," Taylor pleaded.

"I know," Abe said, putting his arm around Taylor. "And we're *going* to help her. We're *going* to get her out of danger. But rushing off to do it ourselves isn't the way. I've been thinking; we need to stay calm and work something out."

"'Work something out'?" Jake mocked. He couldn't

believe he was talking to his dad this way, but he was too angry to care. He thought Abe would be happy. Jake thought that Abe would want to get back to Mom straightaway.

Abe bridled. "Jake, would you please listen to me? We can't go get your mom now, even if she wanted us to. A snowstorm's coming—I can feel it in the air, and from the way the animals are acting. We'll get caught in it if we try to go anywhere now."

"What are you talking about?" Jake shouted, picking up a stick and flinging it off into the darkness. "You have a sixth sense now? It's not even snowing! Admit it. You're scared. Scared to face Mom after you ran off and abandoned us!"

There was silence for a long time.

Abe jabbed the fire with a stick, sending up a flurry of sparks. He took a deep breath. "Look, boys, I love having you both out here with me. Leaving you all those years ago was selfish. I realize that now. But living in the wild with my family was always the big dream. When I first married your mom, it was *our* big dream."

"So make it happen!" Taylor said. "We just need to go get her!"

"What about what your mom wants. Have you thought about that?" Abe paused and ran his hands through his long hair. "Not long after Taylor was born, something happened that changed your mom's big dream. . . ."

"What, Dad?" Jake demanded.

"Taylor got sick, and I went out to find some herbs to treat him with. Your mom wanted to take him to the doctor, but I knew it wasn't that serious. I wanted to do things *my* way, *nature's* way. And while I was out in the wasteland, I . . ." Abe coughed, embarrassed. "I disturbed a copperhead and got bit."

So that was where their dad's strange scar had come from. "But you didn't die," Jake said.

"No, but I nearly did. Your mom called 911 when I didn't come home. I woke up in the hospital. The moment I saw the look on her face, I knew."

"Knew what?" said Taylor, his voice thick.

"That for her the big dream was over." Abe threw his stick into the fire. "Your mom loves you boys so much. No way was she going to take you away from hospitals, away from civilization. Even though she loves nature every bit as much as me, she loves you two even more."

Jake felt a lump in his throat and tears stinging in his eyes. But he was still furious. Abe's stubborn refusal to compromise had torn their family apart once before, but Abe was still refusing to budge.

Abe looked at the boys. "What did she say when you said you were coming to get her?"

"She said not to come," Jake answered reluctantly. "To stay here with you. But—"

"Exactly," Abe interrupted. "I don't know who these guys harassing her are, but if they're anything like Bull was, they're dangerous. *Very* dangerous. Your mom is smart. If she wants you to stay away, it must be for a very good reason, because I'm sure she's desperate to see you. But more than anything else, she wants to keep you safe."

"We're smart too," Jake insisted. "We can go get her and bring her back here without anyone knowing. Then we'll ALL be safe."

Abe shook his head. "Don't be naïve, Jake. You know I like to do things for myself, but sometimes the only smart thing to do is ask for help. We need to contact the authorities. They'll arrest the guys threatening your mom, and keep her safe. Then she can decide what she wants to do. Either come out here and live with us, or take you boys back to Pennsylvania. I've tried the phone again, and the signal is still down, but it should be back up soon. And if it isn't, after the snowstorm that's heading our way, I'll trek into the village and make some calls there."

"But—" Jake's head was spinning with all sorts of reasons why that plan wouldn't work. Even if the stupid phone did work again tomorrow, if the police got involved, Jake and Taylor would have to tell them about Bull, and the money that they'd taken. Anyway, if it were that simple, Mom would have gone to the police by now.

"That's my final word on the subject, Jake," Abe said.

Jake fumed inwardly. Once again his dad thought he knew best. What did he care, anyway? He'd left their mom years ago, so what did it matter to him if she was dead or alive?

Taylor stood, rubbed his stomach, and put on a fake smile that it hurt Jake to see. "Who's hungry? Let's go eat Thanksgiving dinner!"

"Someone's talking sense at last," said Abe with a weak laugh.

"Cody can have mine," Jake said quickly.

"Look, buddy, would you just—"

"I'm not hungry."

Abe stood, his eyes full of sadness. "Suit yourself, Jake. But I'm going to eat your deer and be thankful that your mother is alive, and that I've been reunited with my two boys. I lost you two once before, and I won't risk losing you again."

That night Jake dozed for brief spells but woke frequently to listen to Taylor's deep breathing on the bed that they shared. He could also hear Abe's snores from across the room. His dad slept under a quilt their mom had made, a bright patchwork creation with no two pieces the same.

As Jake lay awake, the argument he'd had with his dad played back over and over in his head. He didn't know how his dad and Taylor could be sound asleep, knowing that on the other side of the country some thugs were plotting to kill their mother. He couldn't stand how helpless it made him feel, not being able to do anything.

His dad was so sure he was right. But he'd more or less admitted it was a mistake to have chosen his dream over his family. So, what if he was wrong this time too? Jake knew he couldn't take that chance—not with his mom's life on the line. No. He wasn't going to wait around for Abe to do something.

Lying there, Jake made a plan.

Just before dawn he heard Abe get up and stoke the fire in the woodstove. Soon he smelled coffee. Jake pretended to be asleep as he heard the sounds of Abe getting dressed. Finally he heard his dad leave the cabin to check on his traplines. It hadn't snowed overnight—so Abe had been wrong about that, too.

After dressing quickly, Jake shook Taylor. Cody had been snuggled under the blankets and popped his head out between the two boys.

Taylor moaned. "Leave me alone."

"Taylor, wake up," Jake insisted.

His brother rolled toward him. Taylor's sandy hair stuck out in all directions. "What . . . what is it? Is it morning?"

"Not yet, but get up."

"Why?"

"Because we're getting out of here."

Taylor's eyes sprang fully open. "What are you talking about?"

Jake climbed out of bed and stood up. "We're going to get Mom."

"Dad changed his mind?" Taylor asked, sitting up.

"No. He just left to check the traps. We need to be gone before he gets back."

"We're leaving Dad?"

"Yeah."

"Forever?"

"I don't know," Jake said. It was the truth. "You heard Mom's voice, Taylor. She needs us, and if Dad won't go get her right away, then we need to."

"But how?"

"Taylor, we'll figure it out. We did it once, and we can do it again. Besides, we know what we're doing this time, don't we?"

Taylor hesitated. "I guess . . ."

"So, c'mon. We've got to hurry."

Reluctantly Taylor got out of bed, followed by Cody. Working quickly, the boys dug out the backpacks their friend Skeet had given them before they'd found their dad. Unlike when they'd left Pittsburgh, the boys knew exactly what they needed to survive. Jake ticked off the items in his head one by one as he stuffed them into his pack.

Two water bottles. Sleeping bag. Map. Compass. Pocketknife. Portable shovel. First aid kit. Flashlight. Rain poncho. Ground cloth. Extra socks and underwear. Two extra shirts. Rope. Cord. Matches. Ziplock bags. Sierra cup. Knife, fork, and spoon. Two-quart pot. Ax . . .

By the time he'd finished, Taylor was nearly done too, but he seemed to be stalling.

"You have your poncho and warm clothes?" Jake asked.

"Sure," he replied. "Listen, Jake, Dad's gonna be mad. I don't know if this is the right—"

"I don't care if he's mad or not," Jake interrupted. "The only thing that matters right now is Mom."

From its secret hiding place behind their bed, Jake pulled out the bag full of cash they'd taken from Bull. Both boys stared at it for a moment. Then Jake tossed it to Taylor.

The last thing Jake picked up was the notebook he'd bought on their trip to town. It was already half-full of the things they'd seen and done since coming to Wyoming. As he stuffed the journal into his pack, Taylor asked him, "Don't you think we should at least leave a note?"

Jake hesitated.

He didn't leave a note when he left us seven years ago.

But then he tore off a piece of paper from the notebook and gave it to Taylor. "Here, you write it."

Taylor scribbled something on the piece of paper and impaled it on a nail overhanging the cabin's sink.

The two boys hoisted their packs and took one last look around them.

"You ready?" Jake asked.

"Yeah . . . I guess so."

"Coming, Cody?" Jake asked.

The terrier wagged his tail, willing to follow the boys wherever they led him.

With stars still shining overhead, they stepped out of the cabin and into the wild. . . .

7

Morning found the two brothers and Cody sitting on a large lichen-covered rock next to a stream winding through a valley of pines and firs. Ice rimmed the edge of the stream, forming a thin sheet over the shallow water. The boys had pushed hard as they'd climbed the mountain passes that separated their dad's world from their goal—the highway. They'd decided against heading into town and trying to find a ride, in case they ran into anyone who knew Abe. Eventually, their muscles had screamed for mercy, forcing them to stop for a brief rest.

"Do you think Dad will follow us?" Taylor asked, tearing off a piece of venison jerky with his teeth.

"Why would he?" said Jake, chewing some of the tough

meat. "He's where he wants to be, isn't he? He isn't about to admit he's wrong."

"But he loves us . . . loves having us around. He said that last night. He's gotta be worried about us, for sure."

"Yeah? Well, if he cares so much, why did we have to find *him*, huh? If this place is so great, why didn't he come and get *us*?"

"Quit being a jerk," Taylor said, looking down. "He sent us loads of letters—it's not his fault we never got them."

Jake fed Cody another piece of jerky and looked down at the map spread between them.

"Whatever," he said. "Even if he does follow us, we'll get to the highway before him. We had at least an hour's head start, maybe more, and we're almost as fast as he is. You might even be faster."

Usually Taylor would have smiled at that. He didn't now.

Jake gazed down at the map. "Once we get to the road, we should be able to catch a ride. With any luck we can get to Riverton or, better yet, Casper, where we can buy bus tickets. Who knows? With luck we might make it back to Pittsburgh in two days."

"And help Mom," Taylor said. The thought seemed to cheer him up.

Jake smiled. "Right. So let's do it."

They helped each other back into their packs, and

then Jake looked down at their dog, who pranced in circles, raring to go.

"Lead the way, Cody!"

They reached the highway two hours later. The sun lay buried behind a layer of cloud as thick as grease-fire smoke. The cold was really beginning to bite, and by the time they reached the road, the first few flakes of snow had begun drifting down out of the sky.

We're getting out of here just in time, Jake thought. If they'd waited, as Abe had wanted to do, they'd never have been able to leave the cabin.

They found a wide patch in the road that would allow vehicles to pull over, and Jake stuck out his thumb. He wasn't sure if you were supposed to smile at the oncoming traffic or not. On their way out to Wyoming last summer, they'd hopped a freight train, caught a ride with a trucker they'd met at a truck stop, and then stowed away on a tour bus. Hitchhiking, though, he only knew from movies.

"I hope we don't get picked up by someone super-creepy," said Taylor.

Jake had been thinking the same thing. "Did you bring your slingshot?" he asked.

"Got it right here."

"Then, we're covered. Besides, we've got the world's best guard dog, don't we?"

Taylor tried to smile but barely pulled it off.

After ten minutes Jake felt numb and frustrated. The highway was almost empty. The few cars and trucks that passed didn't even slow down to give the boys a glance. The snow was falling faster now.

"Let's put our ponchos on," Jake said.

"Maybe we should start walking," Taylor suggested, glancing over his shoulder.

"Let's give it a few more minutes," Jake said.

Taylor shook his head and sat down on his pack. With his poncho on, he looked like a little tent. Cody crawled under the poncho with him.

Cold and worry gnawed on Jake as they waited.

Dad will have found Taylor's note by now.

Jake expected to see Abe at any moment, running at them, his face full of hurt and betrayal. Maybe he'd have the cops with him. Either way, he'd try to stop them.

He glanced over his shoulder one last time. "Okay," he sighed. "Let's start walking."

"Look!" Taylor yelled.

An old Volkswagen camper van was swerving off the road and slowing down next to them. The two boys sprinted for it, hollering until it stopped.

With a rattle of rusty metal, the VW's side door flew open.

A girl with brown hair stuck her head out. "Pretty cold to be backpacking."

"Uh, yeah," Jake panted. "Can you give us a ride?"

"Where you headin', dudes?" a guy with curly blond hair asked from behind the steering wheel. Jake noted another girl perched in the front passenger seat, also staring at them. They looked like college kids.

"Uh, we were trying to get to Casper," Jake said.

"Cool," said the driver. "We're not going that far, but we can drop you in Riverton."

"Or at the junction to Casper—what's that called?" said the girl in the front seat.

"Shoshoni," answered the girl who'd opened the door.

"Any good to you?" asked the driver.

"Awesome. Is it okay if our dog comes too?"

On cue Cody leaped up into the van. The two girls squealed in unison. "He's so cute!"

Jake took that as a yes.

"Climb in," said the driver. "Just throw your stuff in the back."

Jake and Taylor hauled their backpacks into the camper van and slid the door shut. Moments later the boys and Cody were seated comfortably in the van's main compartment, warm, dry, and trundling noisily down the highway.

"Oh, I'm Brittney by the way," said the girl who'd opened the door. "That's Destiny, and Chase is driving."

"Yo, what's up?" Chase said, holding up his hand. "I ain't gonna ask what you two little dudes are doing, all on your own, miles from the nearest town. None of my business. We all got our road to travel, y'know?"

"Sure," Jake said, not knowing what else to say.

"Just make sure you find yourselves someplace safe and warm to stay tonight? The snow's gonna come down hard and deep."

"Chase knows his snow," said Brittney, giving Jake a wink.

The driver laughed. "That's what brought us out here. Gonna check out the boarding at a place called Meadowlark, up near Ten Sleep."

Jake noticed half a dozen snowboards stacked behind the backseat.

"Nice," he said.

The VW didn't seem to go faster than fifty miles per hour or so, but Jake didn't care. At least they were on their way, putting distance between themselves and Abe's cabin.

"See, Taylor?"

"Huh?"

"I told you this would be a piece of cake."

Taylor shrugged, looking far from convinced. "So far so good, I guess."

Jake yawned, stretched, and relaxed. He closed his eyes and let the thrash metal music blasting from the speakers wash him away for a while.

A loud noise jolted him awake. By the looks on their faces, the others had heard it too.

"What was that?" Destiny asked.

Chase looked over at her. "I dunno, babe, but the van's still going. I think we're okay."

"Uh, guys?" Taylor shouted over the music. "Is there supposed to be black smoke coming out of the back of the van?"

"What?" Chase shouted, turning around while still gripping the steering wheel. "Oh, crap!"

He hit the brakes, and the van swerved onto a wide pull-out on the highway. Chase flung open his door and leaped out of the vehicle. After yanking open the side door, he pushed aside a pile of bags and luggage and pulled a small fire extinguisher out from under one of the seats. He ran to the back of the van and tried to open a rear panel, but jerked his hand back.

"It's hot!" he shouted.

"Well, *duh*, it's on fire!" Brittney shouted.

Taylor and Jake leaped out of the van into the driving snow, and Taylor took off the baseball hat he was wearing. "Here, use this!"

Using the cap as a hot pad, Chase again tried to open the rear panel. This time it sprang open—releasing black smoke, and flames.

"Oh God!" Destiny moaned.

Cody began barking, so Jake picked him up and backed away from the flaming engine.

Chase pulled a pin on the fire extinguisher he was holding and sprayed white foam onto the fire. The flames died immediately, but black smoke kept pouring out of the van.

"What happened?" asked Brittney.

Chase gingerly approached the engine. As the smoke cleared, he peered into it.

"We cooked it. That's what happened," he said, and groaned, pulling out a black wire that had most of its insulation melted off.

Jake set Cody down on the ground, and the brothers drew nearer.

"Can you fix it?" Taylor asked.

Chase flung the wire away in annoyance. "No, can you?"

"Um . . . no."

"The oil warning light's been on for a while. I guess we really were low and the engine overheated." Chase sucked his teeth. "Well, whatever happened, we're not going anywhere for a while."

Jake let out a groan.

While Chase and the girls discussed what they should do, Jake pulled Taylor to one side and rummaged in his bag for the map.

"Now what?" murmured Taylor, staring through the falling snow at a sky as gray as an old photograph. "I knew that rustbucket was a death trap!"

"We keep moving, is what," Jake shot back.

"Look. Riverton's about another twenty-five miles," said Taylor, pointing at the highway on the map. "We could hitch another ride. . . . Or we could go back . . ."

Jake frowned, ignoring Taylor's last suggestion. "It took

us forever to get *this* ride. We might not get another one. And if they call the police for help . . ."

He pointed to the map and said, "We're in the foothills of the Owl Creek Mountains. See? Check out this road here. It looks like it heads almost straight over the mountains and could bring us into Thermopolis. We could walk it."

"It's forty miles, Jake!"

"Yeah, but most of it's along dirt roads. We can cover that in a few days. We've done it before. And there's less chance of Dad or the police finding us."

Taylor looked doubtful but said, "I guess we have to do whatever it takes to get back to Mom."

Back by the smoldering van, Chase was looking downcast. "Van's junked, man. We're gonna have to get it towed back to Jackson."

"Sorry," said Taylor.

"Yeah, sorry," said Jake. "Look, ah . . . we'd better hit the road. We'll call our mom. She can come and pick us up."

Chase just nodded. "Your mom, huh? Whatever you say."

"Thanks for the ride."

Chase waved his hand. "Just wish we could've taken you further. You guys stay warm, okay? There's a big storm on the way, but I'm not going to be boarding anytime soon."

A good three or four inches of snow had already stacked up along the side of the road.

"We'll be okay," Jake said, hoping he sounded convincing.

"Here," Chase said, digging into a duffel bag in the back of the van. He pulled out a pair of thin, metallic thermal blankets, along with two tightly knit wool ski hats. "These are for when you hit the slopes."

"Uh, we're not going skiing," said Jake, "but these'll be great. Thanks."

"What? No skiing?" Brittney said. "Have you ever snow-boarded before?"

Jake and Taylor looked at each other. "Um, no. We've sledded."

"We've got to do something about that."

She reached in to where the snowboards were stacked, and pulled out an old one covered in a graffiti pattern.

"It's a little beat up, but you'll have fun with it. I always did," Brittney said, handing the snowboard to Taylor.

"Thanks!" said Taylor, running his hand over the smooth surface.

"I, uh, guess we'd better get going," Jake said.

"*Namaste*," said Chase solemnly. "May the wind be ever at your back."

Taylor strapped the snowboard to his backpack, and the girls helped them get loaded up. They said their good-byes and began the long walk down the highway, without looking back.

Above them the weather began to close in. Soon the light gray clouds turned a deep charcoal color. Heavy, fat flakes began to fall, kissing Jake's face with deathly cold. As he walked on into the swirling snow and the deepening darkness, he realized it was far too late to turn back now.

Piece of cake, he'd said. His own words echoed in his ears, mocking him.

8

Jake and Taylor walked along the highway for about half a mile, looking out for the turnoff. Not a single car passed them.

"Where *is* everyone?" Taylor said uneasily.

"It's just a quiet stretch, is all," Jake replied.

"I guess even the locals don't come down here much."

To Jake's relief he eventually spotted the turnoff he could see on his map. They crossed the highway and stood by it; a straight, unpaved road, heading north and looking as bleak as the surface of the moon.

"You're sure this is the right one?" Taylor asked.

"I think so," said Jake. "Even if it's not, we've got a compass. We'll figure it out."

As they set out up the track, Jake wondered again if he'd

done the right thing. Around his dad's cabin, where the trees grew thickly, shelter was easy to find. Out here nothing grew but sagebrush and rabbitbrush. There was nothing to shield them from the cold winds that blasted them in the face and made their eyes water.

The hats Chase had given them were warm, but they weren't enough. The snow was coming down fast now, in thick flakes that made it hard to see. *Dad was right*, Jake thought ruefully. The storm was here, and they were walking right into it.

Before long the snow was crusted on their shoulders, and their fingers were numb. Jake could just make out the dim shapes of the Owl Creek Mountains through the constant snowfall, but barely anything else. The road, once a dark smudge, was now completely hidden by white snow.

"I'm cold," Taylor moaned.

"Hang in there."

"We're on the wrong road, Jake! I'm sure of it!"

Jake was sure of it too. He'd been suspecting it for a while but hadn't wanted to say. This was on him. He'd talked his brother into coming and had taken them down a deserted road to nowhere. He wanted to throw back his head and yell for help, but he knew that wouldn't do any good.

"Okay, let's say we are on the wrong road. What do we need to do?"

"Dad would know," Taylor said.

"Well, he's not here," Jake snapped. "It's up to us to find somewhere to ride out the storm."

Jake breathed deeply, trudging through the freezing snow and wrapping up the best he could. "We need to keep our heads together and our eyes open. Shout if you see anywhere we could shelter."

High up in the mountains, the snow had piled up even deeper than it had down by the highway. Only the tops of the tallest sagebushes poked out through the white layer. Jake couldn't see anything that even remotely resembled shelter. He let out a sob of frustration before he could stop himself. Cruelly, the wind seemed to suddenly crank up a notch. It moaned across the landscape and cut right through his clothes. Cody whimpered and huddled between the boys' legs, trying to avoid the chill.

"I wish we had a tent," Taylor said, stamping his feet to stay warm.

Jake was about to tell him not to waste his breath on wishes, but Taylor had given him an idea. About fifty feet away he spotted a shallow dip in the landscape.

"Down there," he told Taylor.

Taylor looked at him like he was crazy. "The snow's even deeper there!"

"I know. C'mon, unless you want to freeze to death."

Cody followed in their footsteps as the boys trudged down into the wash and unslung their backpacks.

"What are we doing?" asked Taylor.

"We're going to build ourselves a snow house," Jake said, pulling on the deerskin gloves Abe had given him, protecting his red-raw fingers from the wind.

"We can't make an igloo!" Taylor yelled. "Where would we start?"

"A snow house is *not* an igloo. Dad told us about them. He made one when he had to escape from the wolves," Jake admitted grudgingly, the wind blowing snowflakes into his mouth. "So they can't be that hard to make."

Taylor was either too tired or too cold to argue anymore. He pulled on his gloves, and using their portable shovel and their hands, the boys began stacking up a giant pile of snow.

It took longer than Jake had expected. Every time they threw snow onto the pile, the wind carried away half of it. With all the exertion, he began to sweat. The dampness on his skin made the icy wind bite all the more painfully.

Finally, after twenty minutes of stacking snow, their pile reached about chest high.

"Grab some sticks and lay them across the top," Jake instructed.

Taylor realized what he was doing. "I've got something even better," he said. He unstrapped Brittney's snowboard from his pack, and positioned it across the middle of their snow pile. "It's like she knew," he said above the howling wind.

"Yeah," Jake huffed, placing two sage branches next to the snowboard.

Once their "rafters" were in place, the boys piled about two more feet of snow on top of them. Jake stood back, panting, and nodded once. "Time to start tunneling," he said.

The boys took turns carving out a cave under the snowboard and sage branches. Even Cody pitched in, digging with his little legs, until the snow sprayed up into the air like a fountain. They dug downward, so that the entrance to their shelter was protected from the wind.

Eventually, exhausted, the boys clambered into their snow house. In the light of their kerosene lantern, their little cave felt almost cozy. The wind still howled and snow was still falling , but now that was *outside*.

"It's *almost* like an igloo," Taylor said sleepily. Cody barked his approval and turned circles on the spot before settling down.

Jake tugged at Taylor's arm. "We can't sleep on the snow floor. Come on. We still have work to do."

The boys lined the floor of the cave with their ponchos, the ground cloth, and the foil blankets, then spread out their sleeping bags. Jake stuck a twig through the snow roof to make a ventilation shaft. Using more dry twigs from the bushes that grew nearby, Taylor managed to start a fire at the cave's entrance, and they made hot tea to go along with their cold meal of biscuits, pemmican, and jerky.

By now the gray pall of evening had spread over the landscape. The snow had eased slightly, but the wind howled like it would never stop. The boys retreated into their shelter and walled up the entrance with snow, leaving another hole for air. Then they crawled inside their sleeping bags, huddling together with Cody for warmth.

Jake hesitated before turning off the light. "Taylor?"

"Hmmh?"

"What I said before, about this being a piece of cake? That was stupid."

"Mmm."

"I'm sorry. I just wanted to get back to Mom, but . . ."

A snore interrupted him. Taylor was already asleep.

The boys slept fitfully that night. The air inside the cave stayed warm enough, but with only thin layers beneath them, the cold seeped through to their bones. The whistles and moans of the wind woke Jake several times, and he could tell Taylor was awake too from the way he tossed and turned.

By the time a dim light filtered into the cave, the boys were stiff and cramped. Despite the uncomfortable night, Jake felt defiant and alive, as if he'd faced up to a test and passed it.

"Dad's cabin was like a luxury hotel compared to this," he groaned, stretching.

"Yeah," said Taylor. "I feel sorry for the Eskimos."

They punched their way out of their shelter to find that the wind had finally died down and the snow had stopped. The storm, though, had left two feet of fresh snow piled up across the bleak landscape, and thick fog prevented them from seeing more than a hundred yards in any direction.

"Where'd the world disappear to?" Taylor asked.

"You got me," said Jake, rummaging through the pockets of his backpack. "Hey, Taylor, where's the compass?"

"Don't you have it?"

Jake unzipped another pocket. "I thought you did." Then he noticed one pocket he'd failed to zip the previous day—the same pocket that had held the compass. His stomach dropped.

"Oh no. Remember when we ran for the van yesterday?"

Taylor shook his head. "Oh man," he complained. "The map won't be much use without a compass, huh?"

Jake didn't answer. He turned away. *I blew it again,* he thought.

"Wait!" Taylor said. "I know! We can look at the sun to find which way to go."

Jake threw his arms up at the sky, where the fog completely hid any sign of the sun. "Maybe when the fog burns off."

Taylor sighed. "Or we could turn back? Follow the road back to the highway?"

For a moment Jake wanted nothing more. But then he imagined a patrol car pulling up, and police asking questions that he and Taylor wouldn't be able to answer. For one horrible second he saw Bull's bones on a morgue slab, covered with a sheet. Jake was angry with his dad but didn't want him to go to jail.

"I say we keep going," he said. "Between the two of us, we should be able to find our way through these mountains to Thermopolis, compass or no compass. What do you say?"

Taylor smiled. "I'm in. We've got to live up to our Wilder name, right?"

Jake slapped him on the back. "Right. C'mon, let's pack up."

After a hasty breakfast of jerky and biscuits, Taylor rescued his snowboard from their shelter, and the boys set off. Guessing which way was north based on their travel the previous day, Jake led. It didn't take long to realize just how big a task he'd taken on.

"Man, this is deep," he muttered, slogging through the layer of white beneath him.

"Yeah, you want me to break trail for a while?" Taylor asked.

"Sure. We can trade off."

"We should make Cody do it," Taylor joked. They both looked back to see the dog trailing behind, content to let the boys do the hardest work.

Despite the deep snow, the boys made decent progress—at first. Without warning, the gulley suddenly ended, forcing them to slog up a steep slope to a ridge above them. They continued following that, but then the ridge abruptly changed directions. They zigzagged along the ridge until finally, after a couple of hours, they stopped and looked at each other with dismay.

"Jake, we're even more lost than we were before," said Taylor.

"Yeah, I know," admitted Jake. "Let's stop for a minute."

Jake spread out the foil blanket for them to sit on while Taylor broke out the last of their deer jerky.

"Do you have any idea where we are?" Taylor asked.

Jake looked all around them. The sun still hadn't shown itself through the fog, so their map might as well have been toilet paper.

"No," he said, "but let's head this way."

Making his best guess, Jake led them up into higher ground, following whatever ravines or contours looked promising.

Soon, as they continued, the land ahead of them rose up much more steeply—almost into cliffs. It took them almost two more hours to reach the summit of the rocky pass. At the top they collapsed on their packs, as tired as they'd ever felt before. Even Cody seemed exhausted.

"What do you think Mom's doing now?" Taylor asked.

Jake looked out at the wintry landscape. He let the question hang in the cold air. The truth was, he didn't want to even imagine an answer—it would be all too easy to think the worst.

As they lay there, the fog eventually began to clear

from the ridge they were perched on. For the first time that day, the sun made an appearance, a silvery orb tracking across the horizon. Feeling the dim warmth on his face, Jake opened his eyes, then stood up to get his bearings. Taylor joined him.

Jake realized that they'd actually gone farther west than he'd intended. He began studying the terrain to see which way they should go next, when Taylor exclaimed, "Jake, look! Is that a house down there?"

Jake turned and squinted. At first he saw nothing.

"Right there," Taylor said, pointing.

Then Jake spotted it, a small structure in the canyon below them. The house was too far away to make out many details, but a plume of smoke rose from the chimney into the sky. Jake's spirits rose with it.

"Good spot," he told Taylor. "If we can get down there, we might even find a road—or a ride—to Thermopolis."

"What are we waiting for?" Taylor said, hoisting his backpack.

Jake began leading the way down the opposite side of the ridge. It was steep and soon took a toll on Jake's legs.

It's almost as hard going down as it was coming up the other side.

"I wish we could just sled down to that cabin," Jake said.

He felt a tap on his shoulder and turned around to see Taylor grinning, holding out his snowboard. "Uh, hello? Jake?"

Jake laughed. The snowboard was proving to be their most useful possession. "You wanna go first, so I can watch you fall on your butt?"

"Hey! I'm a pro!" Taylor protested.

Jake helped Taylor get his boots into the snowboard's bindings. The fit was far from perfect, but they managed to tighten the clips, and at last Taylor stood up on the board, ready to give it a try.

"Here goes," Taylor finally said. "Meet you at the bottom."

With Jake's help Taylor pushed off on the board—and did a face-plant into the snow.

Jake cracked up, and Cody ran over to lick Taylor's face. Even Taylor was laughing as he dug himself out of the drift.

"Try again," Jake said, helping him up.

Taylor did, a couple of dozen times. He crashed every way possible. He fell on his face. He flipped over onto his back. He did a three-sixty spin before flopping onto his side. Finally, however, he managed to turn before falling. The next time, he did three turns and went about a hundred feet down the slope.

"About time!" Jake hollered as he and Cody bounded down the slope after him.

The land fell away in a series of steep steps, and at the bottom of the first gradient, Taylor waited for Jake and Cody to catch up with him.

"Your turn, Jake," Taylor said.

"Uh, I don't know, Taylor," Jake said.

"You'll be fine. It's a blast!" Taylor replied as he pulled his boots out of the straps.

But as Jake was about to try, he felt his legs go to jelly.

"Whoa, what was that?" he said, staring wildly at Taylor.

"You felt it too?" Taylor asked. " I thought my legs were just shaky from the ride."

Suddenly the whole landscape began to shift. A deep, low rumble spread through the mountain. It shook the snow-covered ground and seemed to come right up out of the earth and through Jake's legs. And that was when Jake finally saw it—a hundred-foot-wide shelf of snow breaking free right above where they were standing!

Jake yelled, "Taylor, run! It's an avalanche!"

9

Jake and Taylor grabbed their packs and tore down the mountainside. Jake looked behind him frantically and saw a long wave of snow billowing up and coming thundering down toward them.

"Move!" he screamed.

"I'm trying!" Taylor shouted, tumbling through the snow, with Cody fast on his heels.

Jake fled, pure terror powering his limbs, as the mountain seemed to collapse from under him. He snatched up Cody and sprinted, but the knee-high snow slowed him down like thick mud.

It was no use. The avalanche was bearing down on them. In moments they'd be engulfed.

"Taylor, if you go under, make a space for—"

But before Jake even had a chance to finish, the colossal mass of snow smashed into them from behind. Jake staggered, stumbled to his knees, and fell hard. From under his arm Cody let out a frightened yip of pain. Jake gasped for air and flailed with his free hand like a drowning swimmer, but he found nothing. Cody slipped out of his arms and bounded away as the snow heaped up on Jake, burying him alive.

The wave passed, and the earth was still. Cold snow pressed in all around Jake until he couldn't tell which way was up and which way was down. He tried to move his arms, but they didn't budge. The darkness was total. Snow stifled him like a pillow held across his face.

Don't panic, he told himself as he tried to gather a breath. Instead of air he sucked in a wad of frozen snow. Not panicking was easier said than done. Jake racked his brain, desperate to find a way out.

Suddenly a flash of inspiration came to him and he remembered exactly what he had to do—even if it was gross. He gathered the saliva in his mouth and pursed his lips, letting it dribble out. Instead of going down his chin, the spit seemed to be traveling upward, ending up in his right nostril.

I'm upside down.

With a grunt and a heave, he flexed his legs and kicked upward. Suddenly they broke free, and instead of tight snow and compacted ice, Jake could feel the cold air whip across his ankles. Working his elbows back and forth, he struggled upward, wriggling his way out of the snow backward.

Dazed, he got to his feet and looked around him. His backpack was lying half-buried in the snow twenty feet away, but that was the only thing he recognized. Everywhere around him, pure white snow had wiped out the landscape.

"Taylor!" Jake called. Panic was battering his chest and demanding to be let in. "Taylor, are you okay?"

A furry, brown-and-white head popped up from the snow.

"Cody!" Jake yelled. The little dog struggled up, shook himself off, and bounded over. "Good boy! Find Taylor. You got it?"

Cody seemed to understand. He skittered back and forth in the deep snow, sniffing and whining.

"Taylor!" Jake shouted at the top of his lungs. The noise echoed across the mountainside, with no reply.

Jake remembered where Taylor had fallen, but now hundreds of tons of snow had rearranged the hillside, and nothing looked the same. He scrambled up the slope, praying he'd see Taylor's sandy brown hair sticking out of the powder, but there was only blank whiteness in every direction.

On impulse Jake stopped to dig a hole, thinking some deep instinct might have led him to his brother. But there was nothing. He moved a few feet away and dug another one.

"Taylor!" he yelled over and over again, his throat growing hoarse.

He's running out of air, whispered a panicked voice in his mind. *He won't last long. . . .*

Jake smothered the voice, forced himself to think clearly. He racked his brain, and another thought came to him. *What if he was swept past me?*

He whirled to look down the slope for his brother. There was no sign of Taylor, but a figure was emerging from the house they'd seen before. It was a girl, around his age. She had long black hair tied back and was dressed for the cold. The avalanche had pushed him a lot closer to the house.

"Help!" he hollered, waving madly. "Help!"

She cupped her hands to her mouth. "You okay?"

"My brother's buried in the snow!"

The girl sprinted back into the house. Seconds later she emerged with a mop and a broom, and hurried up the slope toward Jake.

"Did you see where he went down?" the girl shouted as she approached.

"Somewhere here!" Jake waved at where Cody was running back and forth.

"Here," the girl said, thrusting the broom into Jake's hands. "You take that side, I'll take this. We'll track across the snowfield and stick the broom handles down into the snow until we find him. Got it?"

The pair of them began crisscrossing the snowfield,

jabbing, moving, jabbing again. Jake wished he had the girl's steady confidence.

On their second pass the girl hit something hard, and Jake's heart leaped into his throat, hoping it was Taylor. They quickly dug down to find Taylor's backpack—but no Taylor.

"We've got to find him!" Jake yelled, plunging the broomstick into the snow.

"Hey!" the girl said, narrowing her eyes. "Keep it together and carry on searching, okay? If he's got an air pocket to breathe in, he'll be fine."

If, Jake thought. He drove the broom handle into the snow again and again. *But what if he doesn't? Hi, Mom, glad you're still alive, but unfortunately I got Taylor killed.*

Suddenly Cody began barking thirty feet up the slope.

"Over there!" Jake shouted.

They scrambled up to find the terrier digging into a deep snowdrift. Jake and the girl dove in to help. Jake plunged his hand into the snow and felt something—*a leg!*

"We got him!" Jake shouted. Together they dug down to Taylor's waist and grabbed a leg each.

"On three," the girl ordered. "One, two . . ."

With a heave they dragged Taylor out. He wasn't moving. Jake fell to his knees next to him.

"Taylor, come on, it's going to be okay. We got you. Taylor, wake up, *please*!"

But Taylor didn't reply. His skin had turned waxen and his eyes were closed.

The girl leaned over Taylor. "Let's get him back to the house, *now!*"

Jake put Taylor over his shoulder, fireman style, took a few steps, and collapsed under the weight.

"Let me help," the girl said. They each took one of Taylor's arms and tried dragging him, but it was slow going as his body sank into the snow. If only they had a sled . . .

Jake suddenly had an idea. He pulled out the poncho from Taylor's pack and spread it on the snow.

"Can you help me get him onto that?" Jake asked. Working together, he and the girl maneuvered Taylor onto the poncho. Then, each taking hold of the poncho, they pulled. Jake held his breath—would it work?

It did! The poncho glided easily over the snow, and in no time they slid Taylor down the slope, all the way to the front door.

They carried him inside and lay him down next to a woodstove in the living room. The girl knelt down and felt for Taylor's pulse.

"He's still breathing," she said. "And his pulse is pretty good."

"Taylor, can you hear me?"

Nothing happened at first. They were the longest minutes of Jake's life, as he gnawed his lip and prayed that his brother would wake up. Then, just when Jake had begun to give up hope, Taylor's green eyes fluttered open, and a loud hacking cough rumbled from his chest.

"Taylor, are you all right?" Jake shouted, feeling the relief course through him.

Taylor swallowed and muttered, "Wh-why are you yelling? I'm right here, you idiot."

The girl laughed and looked across to Jake. "He sounds all right to me!"

A half hour later Taylor sat in a chair next to the woodstove, two blankets wrapped around him, a cup of hot cocoa in his hands. Jake perched in a chair next to him, only taking his eyes off his brother to glance at the room around them.

The house was about twice the size of Abe's cabin, and much more modern. It also had more conveniences, including running water, a refrigerator, and electric lights—powered by a gas generator, Jake guessed. The whole setup seemed luxurious compared to what the boys were used to.

"Here you go." The girl handed Jake his own cup of cocoa and pulled up a chair next to Taylor. She wore a T-shirt and jeans embellished with sequins. "How're you feeling, Taylor?"

"Better." Taylor smiled through a cocoa mustache. "I'm finally getting warm."

"That's good. It might take a while. I'm Kim, by the way."

"You live here by yourself?" Taylor asked.

Kim shook her head and laughed. "Mom's out visiting the cousins. She won't be back till later. So, Taylor, Cody, and . . ."

"Jake," said Jake.

"You two are brothers, right? I can see it in your faces."

"Yeah, we are. So what?"

Kim gave a low whistle. "Whoa! Easy, there."

"Sorry." Jake fidgeted uneasily. He knew he was acting like someone with something to hide, and the girl clearly knew it too. He'd gone outside and retrieved Taylor's backpack as well as the snowboard, but he hadn't thought up a cover story.

With a broad grin she asked, "Sooo, what brings you guys out here on your own, miles from town, just after a giant snowstorm?"

"We're snowboarders," Jake answered, saying the first thing that came into his head.

"Snowboarders!" she echoed. "With only one board between you. So do you, like, take turns?"

"I dropped mine in the avalanche!" Jake protested.

Kim made a noise halfway between a snort and a laugh. "We don't get many snowboarders around here. You do know you're on the Wind River Reservation, don't you?"

The question left Jake tongue-tied, but Taylor stepped in. "We kind of got lost. When we saw your house, we decided to come and ask for directions."

At least that part's true, Jake thought.

Kim just shrugged. "Whatever. It's my mom's job to look after this part of the reservation. I couldn't care less what you guys are up to, but she'll definitely want to know."

A question came to Jake's lips then, as he noticed what

was missing from the house, but he bit it back. Kim must have guessed what was on his mind, though, because she said, "Dad doesn't live with us. Not anymore."

"Our parents split up too," Taylor said.

"Sucks, doesn't it?" Kim said with a wry twist of the mouth.

Jake relaxed a little. Now that they had something in common, maybe she'd stop with the questions.

"So, who do you need to call?" said Kim, standing up. "Your mom, or your dad? You'll want to tell them you're safe, I bet."

Or maybe she'll just ask us more questions. Jake avoided her eyes. "We, uh . . ."

"I'll get the phone. What's your phone number?"

Jake and Taylor glanced at each other.

"We don't, uh, know," Jake said.

Kim burst out laughing. "Oh, give me a *break*! You don't know your phone number? You're out here alone, with a bunch of camping gear and a single freakin' snowboard, and now you've got amnesia, too?"

A sound came from outside—a vehicle was approaching the house.

"That'll be Mom," Kim said. "I'd tell her you are my guests . . . if I knew who the hell you two really were. But maybe you'll tell her yourselves."

"You want the truth?" Jake erupted. "Fine. We've run away from our dad, and we're trying to get to our mom. She's in trouble."

"What kind of trouble?"

"Big trouble. The kind that could get her killed," Taylor said. "She nearly died once already."

Jake sighed. *Geez, Taylor. Tell her everything, why don't you.*

Kim stared at the two of them. Outside, boots crunched on the ice, coming closer to the door.

"I *knew* you were runaways," Kim said, sounding satisfied. "Sorry, guys, but my mom needs to know."

"Don't!" Jake pleaded. "We can't go back to Dad. Our mom needs us. Please!"

Kim gave him a calculating look. She seemed to be weighing her options. Jake gripped the arms of his chair, sick with dread.

A key turned in the door. It swung inward.

There was a pause. Then a worried-sounding voice called: "Kim? Is someone here with you?"

Jake sat, bracing himself for Kim's answer, waiting for the worst. . . .

10

The woman standing in the doorway had Kim's round face and deep-set eyes. She wore a richly colored wool overcoat that hung almost to her knees, with designs of moose and other animals woven into it.

"This is Jake, and this is Taylor," Kim said. "They're in the school wilderness club. We were going to go fishing together, but we, um, played in the snow instead. We had to dig Taylor out of a snowdrift."

Jake exhaled loudly. He suddenly realized he'd been holding his breath.

Kim's mom sighed, shut the door, and hung up her coat. "Kimama, why don't you ever *tell* me when you've invited your friends over? We'll have to have the salmon tonight, and you know I was saving it."

"Mom, don't—"

"Your friends are always welcome, but I need to know in advance. Last time, I came home to your rock band rehearsing in my own living room! Would it kill you to ask permission once in a while?"

Kim rolled her eyes. "I did tell you! I told you last week, remember?"

"Huh?"

"You were on the phone. You probably didn't hear."

There was something a little disturbing about how easily Kim was lying to her mom, Jake thought. She'd clearly had a lot of practice.

"We don't want to be any trouble," he said, feeling guilty.

"It's no trouble," the woman said, looking right through him. "Jake, you said? Kim's never mentioned you before."

"Um, we only moved here recently," Jake said helplessly.

"Mom, give them a break," Kim said, sounding weary. "Is it okay if Jake and Taylor sleep over?"

For the first time the woman smiled at Jake. "I'm Haiwee. Of course you're welcome to stay the night. As long as your parents are okay with it."

"They already called their mom and asked for permission," Kim said quickly.

"Great. Best not to go out in this weather," said Haiwee, "especially after getting stuck in the snow. Tomorrow, once the plow's opened the roads back up, I'll drive you straight down to Riverton."

"Thanks!" Taylor beamed. "So . . . can we still go fishing tomorrow?"

Jake just laughed and rolled his eyes at Kim.

The boys awoke the next morning to a fog of heavenly smells—frying bacon, eggs, toasting bread.

And fried potatoes? Jake asked himself, still lying on the floor in his sleeping bag. He opened his eyes and sat up.

Haiwee glanced over from a small propane range next to the sink. "You're awake," she said cheerfully. "Did you get some rest?"

"Yeah," Jake muttered, rubbing his eyes. Taylor also stirred next to him, but Cody sat over by the range, keeping a careful eye on Haiwee's cooking.

Kim burst through the front door carrying half a dozen pieces of firewood. "Here you go, Mom. I split the logs. Is breakfast ready?"

She began to enter the room, but Haiwee snapped, "Those boots are caked with snow! Go clean them off!"

Kim rolled her eyes. "It must have snowed another six inches last night," she said as she stomped her boots free of snow.

Haiwee tutted. "If that's true, that plow might not get the road open today after all."

"That's okay," Kim said, leaning on the table. "Jake,

Taylor, and Cody can just stay an extra night, right?"

"Hmm," Haiwee answered. "Maybe. But first things first. Who's hungry?"

Taylor sat up suddenly, like an electric jolt had passed through him. "I am!"

Everyone laughed.

"Yes, well, the cold mountain air can give you an appetite," Haiwee told him.

Jake wasn't sure if it was the avalanche, or months of eating lean meat and roots, but he and Taylor ate so much, they thought they might burst.

"You look like you haven't eaten in about a year," Kim said, and laughed.

"We've eaten," Taylor said. "Just nothing as good as this."

Haiwee said, "You can thank me by cleaning up."

Jake kept his eyes trained on Haiwee's face. She clearly had something on her mind, but for now she was keeping it to herself.

"Seeing as how you're stuck here with us, why don't we go fishing like we were going to yesterday?" Kim asked. "It'll get us out of this house, at least."

Jake didn't want to hang around—they were meant to be getting back to their mom as quickly as possible—but Kim gave him a look that told him he didn't have any choice.

Taylor stuffed one final forkful of eggs into his mouth. "Awesome."

"Just try not to start any avalanches, okay?" Kim laughed.

Jake and Taylor looked at each other sheepishly.

"Oh, no," Haiwee said. "You two can go, but Taylor can stay right here. I'm not about to let him go out into the cold again. He's looking pale, and I want to keep an eye on him."

"Aw, I feel great, though. Especially after that breakfast!"

"I'm sorry, young man. The answer is no."

Taylor sighed. "Okay. Jake probably wants some time alone with Kim anyhow."

Jake kicked him under the table. Taylor scowled but knew enough to keep his mouth shut.

Outside the house, Jake waited, hopping from one foot to the other. From behind him he heard the roar of an engine. He spun around to see Kim, driving up on a large snowmobile, a big grin on her face. She stopped next to him.

"Hey there, runaway. Want a lift?"

Jake climbed on board behind her. "Not so loud! What if your mom hears?"

"She won't. Not over this." Kim revved the engine a couple of times. "Sweet ride, huh?"

"Is it yours?"

"Course it is. In case you hadn't noticed, we do live in Wyoming. How else do you think we get anywhere in the winter?"

Kim hit the throttle. Jake's face froze with the wind whipping over him, but he didn't mind. It felt like freedom.

"Dad wouldn't let us have one of these," he called to Kim over the noise of the engine.

She laughed. "So how do you get around? On a horse?"

"We walk."

"Seriously? Man, even the Amish have horses. Your dad must be a real hard-ass."

He is, Jake thought. "It's kind of primitive, I guess," he admitted. "We don't even have electricity in our place, not like you guys."

"You have toilet paper, though, right? Actually, no, don't tell me. I'd rather not know."

Jake's cheeks burned with embarrassment. He felt a stab of jealousy too. Kim and Haiwee were living out in the wild, but they weren't isolated like Abe. Kim even got to go to school and have friends. She was in a band. Meanwhile, Jake and Taylor got to boil up balsamroot.

As they rode, Jake could feel new anger boiling up inside at how rigid and uncompromising their dad had been.

Abe had talked about how glad he'd been that the boys had come to find him. But the truth was, he hadn't adapted his Spartan lifestyle in any way to accommodate Jake's and Taylor's needs. As far as Jake's dad was concerned, it was his way or the highway. *How selfish can you get*, thought Jake.

Kim drove through a rugged canyon until they reached a pond about the size of a football field.

"There's fish in here?" Jake asked, getting off the snow-mobile.

"A ton of 'em," said Kim. "The tribe dammed up the little spring-fed creek here to provide water for cattle, sheep, and wildlife, but they also stock it with rainbow trout. Lots of the reservation kids fish and swim out here. We're lucky it didn't totally freeze over with this storm."

Jake saw that ice skirted the edge of the pond but only stretched out about fifteen feet. After that, it was cold, clear water.

Perfect, he thought.

Kim laid their poles on top of the snowmobile and opened her tackle box. "You know how to rig a fishing pole?"

"Sure."

"Sorry if I was out of line back there, with the joking and all. I guess your dad must be pretty mean, for you to be running away."

Jake shook his head. "He's not mean. It's just . . . complicated."

Kim laid a hand on his arm and made him flinch. "You don't have to tell me if you don't want to," she said.

"He's just so stubborn," Jake sighed. "You can't change his mind, you know? It's like he's in a cult or something. A cult with only one member."

While they rigged up the fishing poles, he told Kim all about the last five months. He talked her through the whole journey to Wyoming to find their dad, only leaving out the part where Bull was killed.

"You should have heard how my mom sounded on the phone," he said. "She was terrified. We couldn't stay with Dad, not after that."

Kim nodded slowly. "So you're heading to Pennsylvania on foot. Sticking to the back roads . . . staying out of sight. Reminds me of something."

"Outlaws?"

"No. I was thinking more of hobbits? You and Taylor are like Frodo and Sam."

Jake laughed despite himself. "You're crazy, you know that?"

"I'm just jealous," Kim said. "I wish I could get out of here too."

"What?"

"Run away, like you guys."

"You don't like it here?" Jake asked, waving his hand at the surrounding mountains. "You *are* crazy. This place is great. You get to be in the wild but close to town, too."

"It's not the place. It's my mom," Kim said. "She's so nosy. She doesn't give me any privacy whatsoever. She always wants to know what I'm doing and who I'm hanging out with. You were there—you saw what she's like!"

"She seemed nice," Jake said carefully.

"You should meet my dad. He's cool. He lives down in Denver, doing art for computer games."

"How come he doesn't live with you?"

"Because he couldn't stand living out here in the middle of nowhere, obviously. One day I'm just going to pack up and go live in the city with him."

"That's funny," said Jake. "We wanted to come live in the wild with our dad, and you want to go live in the city with yours."

"Yeah," Kim said. "Ironic, isn't it?"

Jake set about baiting hooks with salmon eggs, while Kim picked out a little metallic gold fishing lure. They walked down to the edge of the pond and spread out.

"The trout ought to be pretty hungry," said Kim. "They're trying to fatten up for the winter."

Kim and Jake cast their lines beyond the "ice shelf" rimming the pond, and sure enough, Kim quickly got a nibble. When the end of her pole dipped down a second time, she jerked back on it to set the hook.

"Got him!" she shouted as the line whizzed out from her reel. She steadily brought in the fish, a fourteen-inch rainbow.

"Nice trout!" Jake called, as she pulled it across the shelf of ice. And in the next second, he noticed he had a bite too.

Moments later he had his own fish fight on his hands.

"Loosen the drag!" Kim called across to him. "You've got it set too tight, and he might get away."

Jake quickly loosened the dial that controlled how easily the line could get pulled out from the reel. "I think I lost him!"

He began reeling the line all the way in, but his pole tip dipped again.

"Hey, I think—Oh no! It's caught on something."

Kim was busy with her catch, and Jake was determined not to ask for help. He stepped out onto the ice to test if it would hold his weight. It did, so he took another step forward, lifting his pole in the air to try to free the hook.

It still didn't budge, so Jake took another step. The ice cracked but didn't break. Jake continued waving his pole this way and that, trying to dislodge the lure from whatever it was caught on.

"Crap," he said, and without thinking, took one final step toward the edge of the ice.

From below came a slow, splintering, cracking sound.

An image flashed across Jake's mind. *Bull, screaming as he went over the edge, arms flailing, his face a mask of terror.*

Jake heard Kim's panicked yell of warning a second too late.

With a lurch like missing a step on the stairs, the ice collapsed beneath him. The freezing cold waters of the lake swallowed him up.

11

Jake floundered in waist-deep water. The sudden, screaming cold was unbelievable; it seemed to strip him of flesh, flaying him to the bone.

"You idiot!" Kim shouted from the shore. "What were you thinking?"

Jake tried to turn around. Biting steel currents sloshed at his legs. "I don't know," he gasped.

"Can you get out by yourself?" Kim asked, fuming.

"I-I'll t-try."

Jake tried to lift himself up onto the edge of the ice, but more of the frozen surface broke away under his weight. Acting like a human icebreaker, though, he began thrashing his way forward. Finally he managed to climb up onto thicker ice, where Kim helped pull him the last couple of yards to shore.

"We'd better get you back to the house," Kim said urgently. "You could get sick out here. Maybe even frostbite."

"L-lemme take my b-boots off," said Jake. "Th-they're f-full of w-w-water."

"Leave 'em on," Kim said. "The breeze from the snow-mobile might make your feet even colder."

"The poles—"

"I'll come back for them later. Now *move*!"

"O-o-okay."

As Kim helped Jake to the snowmobile, flecks of snow began to dance down from the sky.

"Great," Kim said. "That's all we need. Get on."

Kim fired up the snowmobile, and they raced back toward the house. The snow-laced wind sliced through Jake as he huddled behind Kim. He shivered as if a broken engine inside him were vibrating out of control.

"K-Kim, I'm sorry . . ."

"Don't talk," she told him. "Save your breath."

Haiwee stepped out of the house as they approached. "Why are you back so soon? What's wrong?"

"Jake fell through the ice," Kim explained, helping him toward the door.

"Quick, get him inside."

Inside the house, Haiwee ordered Jake to strip his soaking clothes off. Kim—to his relief—went to the kitchen to fetch hot water. He couldn't have handled her seeing him naked and shivering.

In moments he was wrapped in warm robes and blankets. The shivering still wouldn't stop.

"You're blue," Taylor said in alarm. "Your face. It's actually blue."

Haiwee looked him over. "He's got a mild case of hypothermia, but it's his toes I'm really worried about. Can you feel this?" she asked, reaching down and squeezing his toes.

Jake shook his head.

"Okay. No feeling in your big toe. That's not good."

"Will he be okay?" Taylor asked, eyes wide.

"Look." Haiwee lifted the blanket and pointed. "See how the toes are kind of yellow and gray, and are all waxy? That's frostnip. It's pretty bad, but I've seen worse. Kim," Haiwee said, turning toward her daughter. "Fill up the—"

But Kim was already a step ahead of her mom. She carried a metal basin half-full of warm water over to where Jake sat, and set it down on the floor in front of him.

"How'd you know to do that?" Taylor asked.

"What, you think this is the first time some stupid boy has fallen through ice around here?"

Haiwee tested the water to make sure it was the right temperature. "You never want to heat up frostbitten tissues all at once," she explained as she lifted Jake's feet and placed them into the warm tub one at a time. "Warm water, never hot. Also, don't try to warm the tissues until you can keep them warm for good."

"Why not?" Taylor asked.

"Having the tissues thaw and then freeze again can do permanent damage."

Sudden needles of pain speared Jake's feet. He yelled and jerked them out of the water. Haiwee gently but firmly pressed them back down. "It's going to hurt for a while. You'll just have to put up with it."

Jake groaned.

"At least you can feel something now," Kim said cheerily. "So quit complaining."

"I guess we're not going to Riverton today, huh?" Taylor said.

Haiwee shook her head. "The roads are still blocked anyway. You'll have to stay another night. I'll call your parents and let them know what's happ—"

"That's okay," Jake said, cutting her off quickly, trying not to grimace as he spoke. "I'll call home and let Mom know we're okay."

Worry gnawed at Jake's stomach. It was almost as painful as the dull ache in his toes. He'd thought they were helping their mother by traveling back to see her, but everything was going wrong. It was taking them forever to get back to Pittsburgh. And if Haiwee found out that they were runaways, they'd never get there at all.

I'm such an idiot for falling through that ice, Jake thought.

Taylor spent the rest of the afternoon in a chair next to the woodstove, watching over Jake anxiously. With his pocketknife, Taylor began whittling a small piece of fire-wood into what Jake guessed was meant to be a bear.

After Jake's feet had regained their full feeling, Haiwee gently dried them, placed cotton balls between his toes, and wrapped his feet in gauze, then went to chainsaw some logs outside. Kim made hot tea and brought Jake books and comics to take his mind off the pain and worry. She had a huge manga collection, including some titles he hadn't even heard of. After months with nothing to read, Jake would have been happy to read a phone directory.

"Thanks again for saving my butt," Jake said. "I didn't know frostbite could set in so quickly."

Kim shrugged. "Like I said, it happens more than you'd think."

"I wouldn't even have known what to do. I probably would have jumped right into a hot shower and ended up getting my feet amputated."

"You're such a drama llama." Kim elbowed him in the ribs. "Anyway, you won't have to worry about things like that from now on."

Jake set the comic aside and looked at her. "I won't? Why not?"

Kim glanced out the window to make sure her mom was still out there.

"Because," she said, lowering her voice, "when you guys leave, I'm coming with you."

12

"Oh no," Jake said. "No way. Forget it."

"Ever since you told me about your mom," Kim said, "I've been thinking about my dad. I've made up my mind, and I'm going to go find him."

"Do you even know where he is?" Taylor asked from his place in front of the fire.

"He's in Denver." Kim glanced at the window again.

"Yeah, but *where* in Denver?" Jake asked.

"I'll track him down. I have his address. I can use Google."

"But you can't just run out on your mom!" Jake said desperately.

Kim gave him an acid look. "Why not? You both ran out on yours."

"That was different!" Taylor said.

"Yeah," Jake picked up. "We could have been killed if we'd stayed in Pittsburgh."

"You could have been killed? So how come it's safe to go back now?"

Because Bull's dead, Jake thought. But he kept his mouth shut and gave Taylor a warning look so he'd do the same.

Just then Jake and Kim spotted Haiwee heading back to the house. All three of them stopped talking. Jake, though, could feel his stomach clench. Although Kim hadn't said so, he knew she could betray them at any time, just by telling her mom that they weren't really friends from the school wilderness club.

The front door opened, and after stomping three or four times on the front step, Haiwee entered and took off her boots. "Still snowing out there," she said, shedding her thick wool coat. "I doubt that snowplow's even going to make it up here tomorrow. How are your toes, Jake?"

"They feel okay, but I don't think I'll ever play the piano with them again."

"Cute. Let's take a look at them."

Haiwee knelt down next to Jake's feet and carefully unwrapped the gauze. She gently squeezed them. "That hurt?"

"They kind of burn a little bit, but not too bad."

Jake glanced across to Kim. She didn't meet his eye. Her jaw was set. The conversation they'd been having still hung in the air between them.

"I think you got lucky." Haiwee nodded. "I can only imagine how worried your parents must be."

"Don't worry," Jake said. "My mom knows we're okay, and I said we'd hopefully be back tomorrow."

Kim glared at Jake. Her eyes silently said, *You'd better not think of leaving without me.*

Taylor picked up Jake's cue. "Yeah, my butt's getting numb with all this sitting around."

"Oh, is that right? I've got a job for you after dinner, then," Haiwee said. "Speaking of which, I'd better deal with that trout."

When Haiwee was out of earshot, Jake whispered, "Thanks for not ratting us out."

Kim shrugged and swept her black hair over her shoulder. "I still might. I haven't decided."

Jake hissed "Your mom's cool. She's been really kind to us. And she loves you. She doesn't deserve this!"

"Yeah?" To Jake's amazement, Kim wiped a tear from her eye. "She's suffocating me, Jake. Just like she smothered my dad. I need to spread my wings, and you can't stop me. I won't let you."

By the time Jake and Kim had finished cleaning up after dinner, Haiwee and Taylor were back at the table, examining some weird wooden loops that looked like homemade fish traps.

"Remember that job I mentioned?" said Haiwee. "Take a seat."

"Look, Jake," Taylor enthused. "These are old snow-shoes!"

Jake sat down. "Really? Oh yeah, I see. They look a little beat up."

"They are," said Haiwee. "My brothers and I used these when we were kids, and I've been meaning to repair them for years. Now I don't have to."

"Why not?" Taylor asked.

Haiwee said, "Because you're going to do it for me."

"You're kidding," Taylor said.

"Nope. See?" she said, squeezing one of the wooden loops. "The hardwood frames are still in good shape. All we have to do is use these strips of moose hide to rebuild the webbing and bindings."

Taylor looked at the bag of rawhide strips sitting next to the snowshoes. "Where do we even start?"

"You don't have to do it if you don't want to," Kim said, and yawned. "She can't make you."

"Kimama!"

"What? It's true. Even way out here there are better things to do than repair ancient snowshoes." She flung her-self onto the couch and began to leaf through the comics.

Jake coughed, picked up one of the strips, and ran it

between his fingers. "So how do we do this? Just tie the strips straight across?"

"No, you want to weave a diagonal crosshatch pattern," Haiwee explained.

"Is that traditional or something?"

Haiwee laughed. "Not really. It's just stronger that way."

Jake and Taylor each took one of the wooden frames, and under Haiwee's instruction began rebuilding the snowshoe webbing one strip at a time. Haiwee stopped Taylor only moments after he'd started. "Not like that, honey. You're threading the strips too tight."

"But they need to be tight, don't they?"

Haiwee showed him where the overtight strips were buckling the frame out of shape. "You've got to see the whole picture, not just what's under your nose. And you need to work *with* the materials, not *on* them."

Jake thought he understood. "So it's like going with nature and not fighting it?"

"You can't fight nature," Kim called from the couch.

As Jake worked, he enjoyed the feel of the moose hide strips in his hands, not to mention the satisfaction of learning a new skill. Weaving the strips in and out was calming, like meditation.

The boys and Haiwee worked steadily. As it grew dark, Kim lit kerosene lanterns. Soon there were several pairs of repaired snowshoes on the table.

Jake's thoughts strayed to his dad. He wished the man

could meet Haiwee and learn from how she lived. His father's whole approach seemed to be about *fighting* for survival—constant alertness, always just scraping by. Every now and then they'd had a glimpse of the poetic side of living out there. But what was the point of it all? The country was just as beautiful when you saw it from a snowmobile. It wasn't cheating to have a gas-powered generator.

After they completed the webbing, Haiwee showed them how to make the bindings for the snowshoes, using a wider strip of moose hide with a thin ankle strap that could be adjusted.

At last they tied their final knots and made the bindings for the snowshoes. Holding one aloft, Haiwee smiled triumphantly. "Well, what do you think?"

"Very cool," Jake said, admiring his own handiwork.

Taylor was only a bit less enthusiastic. "My fingers hurt, but they're pretty neat, I guess."

Haiwee raised her eyebrows. "Only pretty neat?"

"Okay, they're cool."

"Well, I hope you think so," Haiwee said, handing a pair to Taylor, "because they're yours."

"Huh?"

"Are you sure?" Jake asked.

Haiwee smiled. "Oh, yes. They've been collecting dust for a long time, and as you can see, Kim has no interest in them. I think you were meant to have them."

"Wow!" Taylor said. "Thanks."

"Yeah," Jake said. "Thank you."

"Besides," Haiwee continued, "you might need them the next time you find yourself on the side of a mountain! Is it still snowing outside, Kimama?"

"Yep," said Kim, fixing tea over in the kitchen area.

Haiwee frowned. "I was afraid of that. You are welcome to stay here tonight, but tomorrow we've got to find a way to get you home."

"It's fine. Our mom knows we're safe," Jake lied.

"And your dad?"

"Dad doesn't care," Jake said before he could stop himself.

Taylor opened his mouth to argue, but Jake ignored him. "He's got his own stuff going on, and that's all he cares about."

"I'm sure that's not true," Haiwee said gently. "All parents love their children. Why do you think your dad doesn't care about you?"

Kim appeared in the doorway. "Stop being so nosy, Mom."

"That's enough, Kimama."

"I mean it. It's bad enough that you're constantly interfering with my life and telling me what to do. Don't go pestering Jake and Taylor."

"I'm sorry about this," Haiwee told the boys. "She's going through a rebellious phase."

"I am *not* going through a phase!"

Jake shifted uncomfortably in his chair. *This is all*

my fault, he thought. *I should have never opened my big mouth.*

As Kim stood trembling with anger in the doorway, Haiwee went and took her hands in hers. "The reason I want to know what you are up to is because I care about you, even if you find that hard to believe now. I've always been there for you, and I always will be. Even when everyone else lets you down."

Kim shook her mom off. "Don't say that!"

"Your father's not coming back," Haiwee said. "He left us. It was his choice. And you need to make your peace with that."

Jake sat up and stared. He hadn't realized Kim's dad had walked out too.

"He left *you*!" Kim yelled. "You and this stupid, boring, dead-end life! He didn't leave *me*. He still wants to see me again. He wants—"

"Honey, he hasn't been in touch for three years," Haiwee said, and the sadness in her voice was hard for Jake to bear. "He has a new family in Denver. I know you're angry, Kim. I was too, for a long time. But I had to let go. And you need to do the same."

"But why would he just up and leave like that?" Kim demanded. "He didn't even leave a note!"

"Sometimes people do selfish things," Haiwee said. "They do things because they want to, and that's all the reason they need."

Jake glanced over at his brother. Taylor was glaring at him, his face pale, his lips pressed together.

Haiwee's words sank slowly into Jake's heart, and he understood. *We ran out on our dad. What we did to him was no better than what he did to us.*

We left Mom when she needed us most. Now we've done the same to Dad, and it's all my fault.

Jake crossed the room and knelt down by Taylor, who flinched away from him.

"Taylor, listen," he whispered. "I know what you're thinking. We'll make it up to Dad."

"You better," he replied.

"I promise. But we have to get Mom first. We have to make sure she's safe. Then we can make things right with Dad. Okay?"

Taylor bumped Jake's offered fist.

"So when do we leave?"

13

Jake woke his brother before dawn the next morning. Taylor grunted once but didn't complain, and the boys silently dressed and packed their gear, taking care to make as little noise as possible.

"Can't we say good-bye to Kim and Haiwee?" Taylor whispered.

"No. Let them sleep. I wrote them a note."

Taylor weighted the note down with the little bear that he'd carved. "I hope they like it," he said.

The boys hoisted their packs and carried their snowshoes outside, closing the door softly behind them.

Above them the clouds had cleared, exposing a waxing moon that cast a dazzling light over the entire valley.

"Wow!" Taylor exclaimed. "It's like daytime out here."

"Shh," Jake hissed. "It's about twenty degrees colder than yesterday too. My toes hurt."

They strapped on the snowshoes they'd repaired and took their first steps on the snow.

Suddenly the door opened behind them. Jake twisted around, heart fluttering, expecting to see Haiwee standing there. Instead it was Kim.

"Wow. Sneaking out before daylight. That's low."

Cody pranced up to her, wagging his tail.

"Uh, we didn't want to wake you," Taylor lied.

"Yeah, right," said Kim. "You know the deal. I told you I was coming with you. Just give me five minutes to grab some stuff."

Jake took a breath. "Kim, that's a bad idea."

"Oh really?" She cocked her head. "So maybe a better idea is for me to go tell my mom we've got two runaways in the house? She'll be mad that I lied to her, I guess, but I could always say you threatened me."

"You wouldn't do that."

"Try me."

Kim shivered in the cold, and a puff of steam left her mouth. Jake had no idea what to do. She had him trapped.

So he told the truth.

"Kim . . . if you leave your mom now, you'll regret it. I know it seems like the right thing to do. But you'll just hurt her."

"Good!" She barked a cold laugh. "Man, you are such a

hypocrite, Jake. You left your dad, and you don't regret it at all!"

"You're wrong," Jake said.

"What?"

"I do regret it. I wish we hadn't done it." He glanced over to Taylor. "I was stupid and impulsive, and I just wanted to teach him a lesson."

Jake could see that that was exactly what Taylor had thought.

"But it's too late for us. We've got to keep going. It's not too late for you."

Kim's face sagged, and her eyes were wet. She impatiently rubbed them, then nodded.

"It's not fair," she said.

"I know."

"You're both on this big adventure, and I'm stuck here. Trapped in the dullest place on earth. I can't stand it."

"Believe me," said Jake, "it's not an adventure. It's tough."

"Yeah," said Taylor. "And it's scary. I mean, if you hadn't been here, I might be dead now."

Kim didn't say anything for a moment. Then she said, "Will you send me a postcard at least?"

Taylor grinned. "You bet. I left you a little present inside."

Kim pulled the carved wooden bear from her pocket and smiled. "I know. I found it. Thank you." She took a deep shuddering breath and glanced at the sky. "You both better get out of here before my mom wakes up. Do you guys even know where you're going?"

Jake searched the sky until he found Polaris. He pointed northeast. "I'm thinking that way."

Kim stifled a giggle. "Well, you could. But you'll have an easier time if you just walk down the valley here, like we went on the snowmobile yesterday. You can't see it, but there's a road there. Follow it down to Thermopolis."

"Thanks." Jake grinned. "For everything. We'll see you again. I promise."

"Go on, get out of here, you hobbits," Kim said. She waved. "Good luck, Frodo and Sam."

Walking in the snowshoes took some getting used to, but they quickly realized that they never would have made it out of the valley without them.

"Man, these things are great," said Taylor. "There's got to be three, four feet of snow on the ground, but it's like we're just gliding on top of it."

"I wouldn't call this gliding. Scooting maybe," said Jake.

"Whatever. I'm just glad we have them."

Unfortunately, they didn't have snowshoes in Cody's size. The terrier did his best to leap from one giant footstep to the next, but after a quarter mile Jake called a halt.

"What's up?" Taylor asked, looking back.

Jake picked up Cody and placed him in the main compartment of Taylor's backpack.

"Hey," Taylor objected. "Why do I have to carry him?"

Jake grinned. "Consider it payback for almost getting yourself killed in an avalanche."

"Very funny," Taylor huffed, but Cody barked happily from the top of Taylor's pack.

The boys continued moving quickly, trying to keep warm and cover as many miles as possible before Haiwee figured out they'd left. After about an hour they linked up with the road Kim had told them about and, without pausing, pushed east. As they trekked down a larger valley, they passed a few farms, framed by more spectacular mountains rising on either side of them. They heard the haunting hoots of a great horned owl and the frantic yips of a pack of coyotes from up in the mountains. Cody barked back at them.

As the moon began to fade in the dawn sky, the boys finally reached the highway. They walked for another mile before a rancher in a pickup truck stopped and gave them a lift into Thermopolis. As they sat shivering in the open bed of the pickup, Taylor spotted a billboard for a hot spring. Moments later they passed another billboard for a dinosaur museum.

"Hey, Jake, did you know Thermopolis had all this stuff?"

"No," Jake said, "but the name should have been a clue, I guess."

Dawn was just creeping over the town when the truck slowed to let the boys and Cody out. Jake asked if there was a diner open anywhere, and the rancher directed them to a café a few blocks away.

So far so good, Jake thought.

Sure enough, the café was already doing a brisk business when the boys reached it. When they tried to go in, though, the waitress stopped them.

"Sorry, boys, no dogs allowed."

Taylor opened his mouth to protest, but the waitress's hard stare told him it wasn't going to happen. Reluctantly he studied the street and spotted a sign he could tie Cody to. "Okay, boy," he whispered as he knelt down beside the terrier. "You stay here, okay? We'll bring you a nice treat when we're done."

Cody whined.

"It'll be okay," Jake assured Cody. "We'll be right back."

The boys hurried inside and sat down on stools at the counter. Jake's stomach rumbled as he looked over the menu. He tried to remember the last time either of them had eaten in a real restaurant. *It must have been when we were with Sharon and she bought us meatloaf at that diner back in Nebraska.*

Jake recalled with a twinge of regret how nice the trucker had been to them and Cody. She'd laugh if she could see them now, trekking all the way back to where they'd come from.

The boys didn't order every item on the menu, but they got close: Denver omelets, hash browns, bacon, sausage, juice, and toast. Jake made notes in his journal as they stuffed themselves, and even ordered apple pie for dessert. As if on cue, Cody barked excitedly outside. Taylor bundled some food into a napkin for him.

Feeling stuffed to the gills, Jake called the waitress over and paid using some of Bull's money. The waitress gave them a wry grin. "You're sure you boys don't want to order anything else? We still have a little food left back in the kitchen."

"I'm stuffed," Taylor said, beaming and wiping away flaky pastry from the side of his mouth."

"Me too," Jake said. "But there is one thing . . ."

"What's that, hon?" the waitress leaned down to ask.

"Do you know if there are any buses to Riverton or Casper from here?"

The waitress frowned and pressed the end of her pencil into her chin. "There's a Greyhound that stops out at the gas station on the highway," she said, "but not till two p.m."

Jake pursed his lips, considering it.

If we can just get to Riverton, he thought, *we'll be able to get a bus halfway across the country. It would sure beat trekking through snowdrifts.*

The waitress added, "I know that's hours until the bus gets here, but you boys could go take a dip in the hot springs while you wait."

"Sounds good," Taylor said.

Suddenly the waitress frowned, looking out the window.

"What's up," Jake asked.

"That dog of yours," she started. "Wasn't he just out there?"

Jake twisted his neck and looked out at the sidewalk, a feeling of dread stabbing his full stomach.

"Oh no . . . ," Taylor began.

"Cody!"

14

Jake and Taylor grabbed their things and sprinted outside.

"Jake!" Taylor cried, frantically looking in all directions. "Where did he go? Do you see him?"

Jake didn't reply, but his heart was in his throat. He quickly scanned up and down the street but didn't see a trace of Cody anywhere.

"Oh, man!" Taylor cried. "We shouldn't have left him out here alone, Jake! He probably got scared and wriggled his way free!"

Jake knelt down to the base of the sign and saw that the rope Taylor had used to tie up Cody still lay in the snow, intact.

"It looks like he got out of that loop you tied," Jake said.

"What are we gonna do?" Taylor asked, pacing back and forth in the snow.

"What would Dad say if he was here?"

"He'd tell us not to panic."

Jake nodded. "Right. So let's calm down and use our heads."

Taylor took a deep breath and began scanning the snowy ground. "Look," he burst out. "Are those tracks?"

Jake and Taylor hurried to a spot a few feet away. The sidewalk hadn't been cleared yet, and it was still covered by a thick layer of snow. The boys knelt down and, sure enough, found a fresh set of tiny dog tracks heading east—as clear as any deer trail snaking through a forest.

"That's Cody," Taylor exclaimed. "Let's go!"

Hitching their packs as they walked, the boys quickly set off after the terrier. They didn't bother putting on their snowshoes, as most of the slush had been shoveled away from the streets and sidewalks. Fortunately, enough snow remained for them to follow Cody's footprints as they headed across a bridge that spanned the Bighorn River, and then turned north. Jogging now, the boys followed the tracks for another couple of blocks, until they passed a sign reading HOT SPRINGS STATE PARK.

Rising more than a hundred feet high to their right, a dramatic ridge of red rock stretched across the horizon. A few gnarled trees clung to the ridge, along with patches of sagebrush, but mostly it seemed barren and desolate, like the mountains around Kim and Haiwee's place.

"Look at that!" Taylor exclaimed, pointing toward billowing clouds of steam rising up from the ground.

"Must be the hot springs," said Jake.

The boys hurried over to a twenty-foot-high slimy lump of rock with water streaming down from the top of it.

"What the heck is this thing?" Taylor asked.

"I think the minerals from this hot springs built it up," said Jake. "It's all made from calcium or something like that."

Taylor wrinkled his nose. "It stinks like rotten eggs."

"Sulfur from the hot springs," Jake explained. "Still want to swim in it?"

Taylor was about to answer, when instead he shouted, "Hey, Jake! There he is! Over there!"

Jake spun around to see Cody in the middle of a large group of kids gathered outside a building a hundred yards away. A sign next to the building read MUSEUM in giant letters, and two full-size motor coaches stood parked in the parking lot nearby.

"C'mon!" Taylor yelled, rushing toward the building. Jake ran after him.

When they reached the crowd, Taylor pushed his way through to Cody, who was wagging his tail and soaking up attention from a dozen students.

"There you are!" he cried, squatting down to wrap his arms around the dog.

Jake also made his way through the crowd, relief washing through him.

"You had us worried!" Jake good-naturedly scolded Cody, as he knelt down to pet him.

"Is this your dog?" a redheaded boy asked. A second, almost identical redhead stood next to him.

"Yeah," Taylor said. "He decided to go exploring."

"He's cool," said a girl with short brown hair and pink glasses.

"Yeah, he's all right," Jake muttered, rubbing Cody behind his ears.

"What are you guys doing here?" Taylor asked, straightening up while keeping an eye on Cody to make sure he didn't take off again.

"We're from Madison Junior High School. I'm Max, and this is my brother Marty," Max told them.

"Let me guess," Jake said, reading his Bulls sweatshirt. "Chicago?"

"Yeah," said Marty. "We came out here to Casper for a band competition, then drove out here to Thermopolis for the dinosaur museum."

"Did you win?" Taylor asked.

The girl with the pink glasses scrunched her nose. "No. Robby dropped his clarinet during our final number and then knocked his music stand over trying to pick it up."

"It wasn't his fault, Tess," insisted one of the twins. "Lucy poked him in the butt with her trombone slide."

Jake and Taylor laughed.

"So, what about you guys?" Tess asked.

Fortunately, before they answered, a portly woman with curly black hair stepped out of the museum building. "Okay, everyone, listen up! We've paid for all of you, so you can go in, but remember, we only have an hour before lunch, so don't waste any time."

Excited murmurs swept through the students, and they began filing into the building.

"Well, thanks for catching our dog," said Jake, turning away.

"Hey, do you want to come in with us?" Max asked.

"Yeah, Jake! Let's do it!" Taylor said. "Our bus doesn't leave for hours. C'mon, please?"

Jake hesitated. Was it really safe to leave Cody again?

"*Please*, Jake," begged Taylor. "It's a dinosaur museum!"

With Taylor, the twins, and Tess staring at him, Jake couldn't say no. Besides, hanging out with a group of kids would help them blend in more.

"Just watch out for Mrs. Ratzlaf," Marty warned him, pointing at the heavyset woman. "She's a *demon*."

Taylor tied Cody outside—more securely this time—and gave him the bundle of food from the diner. The two boys left their backpacks and snowshoes behind the ticket counter and did their best to blend in with the schoolkids pouring into the museum.

All around them stood incredible fossils and replicas

of some of the most amazing animals ever to walk the earth. As the boys joined the class on the museum's "Walk through Time" tour, Taylor started calling off names left and right, from allosaurs to *T. rexes*, velociraptors to *Microraptors*.

After hearing Taylor spit out another half dozen dinosaur species, Max and Marty grinned. "I guess you must be a superbrainiac," Max said.

Taylor blushed. "Me, a brainiac? No way."

"He's just got a special thing about dinosaurs," Jake explained to the twins.

Later, they paused at a special exhibit of Stone Age tools, and Max let out a whistle. "Man, I'm glad we don't have to live like cavemen did."

"Yeah," Marty said. "It would have been a nightmare. Hunting for your food. No computers. No video games!"

Max laughed. "No breakfast cereal. Imagine getting up in the morning and you've got to go pull the guts out of a deer, or whatever."

I don't have to imagine it, Jake thought.

"You know, some people still live like that now," Jake said.

"Really," Marty said, confused. "That must suck."

Jake looked away, embarrassed. Even though it *did* suck sometimes to live like that, he suddenly felt defensive. It wasn't Max's and Marty's fault. They didn't know all the things Jake and Taylor had seen or been through. But their ignorance still stuck in his throat.

After the museum the band members went to a local pizza place for lunch—the only place in town big enough to handle all of them. Jake and Taylor tagged along, again leaving Cody tied up outside. Despite inhaling a huge breakfast, Jake and Taylor demolished half a pizza each. It felt just like being back at school with their friends, and soon Jake and Taylor had completely let their guard down.

Watching Taylor wolf down a third of a slice of pepperoni in a single bite, Tess said, "You guys are human garbage disposals. How do you stay so skinny?"

Hiking over mountains, Jake thought. *Digging out of avalanches. Walking miles in snowshoes.*

Taylor waved away the question. "We get a lot of exercise."

Jake had to grin at that. It was true, after all.

As Max was chewing his last mouthful of pizza, he nudged Jake. "Uh-oh, Ratzlaf is coming!"

"Let's go, Taylor," said Jake.

The pair of them stood up, ready to make a break for it, but the rotund curly-haired band instructor was already moving across the floor, making a beeline for their table. If they left now, they'd just draw even more attention to themselves.

"What do we do?" Taylor asked out of the corner of his mouth.

"Sit down. Just act normal."

Jake and Taylor sat down again, hunched low in their seats.

Mrs. Ratzlaf stood at the end of the table. *She looks like an army sergeant,* Jake thought.

He glanced up at her before he could stop himself. There was an enormous mole on her chin. He couldn't take his eyes off it.

"Look at this mess," Mrs. Ratzlaf said, sounding revolted. "What a bunch of animals. You are *not* acting like ambassadors for your school."

A few students mumbled "Sorry," but most said nothing, choosing instead to hang their heads in guilty silence. Jake and Taylor stared at their plates.

Mrs. Ratzlaf started to shuffle around the table toward Jake. He could practically feel her hot breath on his neck.

"Finish up, all of you," she said from behind him. "Our bus leaves in fifteen minutes."

Jake reached for his Coke and took a noisy, rattling slurp. *Act normal,* he told himself. A bead of sweat ran down his forehead and caught in his eyebrow. It tickled.

Across the table he saw Taylor swallow hard and lift a slice of pizza to his mouth. Taylor's eyes kept flicking up to above Jake's head, where Mrs. Ratzlaf loomed over him.

Jake couldn't stand it. He wanted to run.

In the next moment a heavy hand clamped down on

his shoulder. Mrs. Ratzlaf's huge head leaned over. Her eyes glared into his.

"And who might you be, young man?" she demanded. "You're not in my band, that's for sure. Where are your parents?"

Jake's throat locked up. He couldn't say a word.

The woman leaned in so close that Jake could smell her sour breath. "I think we'd better have a little chat."

15

Taylor looked at Jake, panic darting across his features. Marty and Max looked his way too as he began stuttering a reply.

"Uh, well, we were—"

"Mrs. Ratzlaf, don't you remember?" Marty jumped in. "They were in the band from Denver that got second place in the jazz competition."

The band director's eyes narrowed, looking from Jake to Taylor and back again. Jake held his breath. Any second now she'd call the police, or at least kick them out of the restaurant.

Mrs. Ratzlaf sagged, doubt creeping across her face. "Huh. I thought you looked familiar."

Max added, "Jake plays trumpet and Taylor plays alto sax."

Mrs. Ratzlaf brushed him off, irritated. "Of course, I

remember now. Congratulations on your second place. What I don't understand is what you're doing *here*?"

"Uh, after the competition," Jake picked up, "our parents decided to bring us to Thermopolis for a day."

"Yeah, we've been wanting to come for a long time," Taylor added.

"Our mom and dad are still back at the dinosaur museum," Jake lied, "but when we ran into Max and Marty, they said we could hang out with you guys for a while."

He stopped himself before he gave in to the temptation to keep talking.

"I suppose there's no harm in that," Mrs. Ratzlaf said. "I just want to make it clear that we are not responsible for either of you. Understood?"

"Yeah, sure," Jake said, trying to look innocent.

"Right. Anyway, don't dillydally."

Mrs. Ratzlaf continued on to the next tables, telling everyone to get a move on.

Marty looked at the others. *"Dillydally?* What century is she living in?"

The others chuckled, but Jake and Taylor sighed with relief. "Thanks for covering for us," Jake said.

"Yeah," said Taylor. "That was a close one."

"So," Max said, "when are you going to tell us the *real* deal?"

"Uh, what do you mean?" Jake hedged.

"Well, obviously you aren't in a jazz band from Colorado,"

Max said. "And your parents aren't back at the museum. So what *are* you doing here on your own?"

"Are you orphans?" Tess asked excitedly.

"No!" Taylor exclaimed. "We're going to rescue our mom."

"Why? Is she in trouble?"

"Yeah . . . Well, no . . . We don't know," said Taylor all at once.

"Well, which one is it?" asked Marty.

Jake and Taylor looked at each other. Neither of them answered.

"Maybe we can help you," said Max. "We'd want help if *our* mom was in trouble.

"We might as well tell them," Jake said, sighing.

They gave the twins and Tess a quick rundown of the last five months. They left out plenty of details—like seeing Bull shoot the man back in Pittsburgh, and how Bull fell to his death in Grand Teton National Park. But they did tell their new audience that some bad people might be after their mom and that was why they had to hurry back to Pittsburgh.

When they'd finished their story, Marty whistled. "Whoa. You guys are like outlaws."

"They're more like explorers," Tess said.

"I'm sorry about your mom, but I wish *we* got to do stuff like that," Max chimed in. "Plus, you don't even have to go to school!"

"You know, back at the museum you said life in the wild

must suck," Jake reminded him. "Now you're jealous?"

"Oh . . . Sorry." Max looked sheepish. "You just make it sound so cool."

"It's not as cool as you think. It's dangerous. You were right about that part."

"Yeah," said Taylor. "Just a couple of days ago, I got caught in an avalanche and Jake and Cody had to dig me out."

"An avalanche? Seriously?" Tess stared at Taylor like she was sitting across from a rock star. In the next moment Mrs. Ratzlaf's voice boomed through the restaurant.

"FIVE MINUTES, EVERYONE! If you have to use the restrooms, do it NOW! We're not stopping again between here and Nebraska!"

"Quick," said Taylor. "Do any of you guys have a cell phone? We want to try to call our mom to see if she's all right."

"Good idea," said Jake.

"Yeah, sure." Marty pulled a phone from his pocket and handed it to Jake.

The boys hurried outside to where Cody was waiting. Taylor slipped him half a slice of sausage pizza that Tess hadn't finished, while Jake dialed their home number. Unlike their call on the satellite phone the week before, the sound on Marty's phone came through loud and clear.

"Is she answering?" Taylor asked.

Jake shook his head. "Not yet."

"Hang up and try again," Taylor said, but just then a voice spoke.

"Hello?" their mom said nervously.

"Mom! It's me, Jake!"

"Oh, thank God!" Jennifer said, her voice filled with relief. "Are you boys all right? I've been so worried about you since we got cut off last time. Where are you?"

"It's okay, Mom. Taylor, me, and Cody are fine. We're on our way back to Pittsburgh. Are *you* okay?"

Jennifer hesitated on the other end of the line. Then she said, "Yes. I'm fine. Don't worry about me."

Taylor had his ear close to the phone but pulled back. *Something's wrong,* he mouthed to Jake.

Jake nodded. "Mom, what about Bull's boss's men? Did they come to see you?"

"Is Bull with you?" Jennifer asked, alarm in her voice. "Did he hurt you boys?"

"No, Mom. We've haven't seen Bull in . . ." The words caught in his throat. "Months."

Because he's dead, Mom. DEAD.

"These men," Jen whispered. "They think Bull stole some money from them."

"What men?" Jake said, worried now.

"Bull's business partners!" she said. "They tell me different things every time."

Jake thought back to the night Bull shot the guy in the woods near their home in Pittsburgh. Bull had obviously been mixed up with some very bad people. It had been naïve to think that just because Bull had disappeared, these people would let the matter drop.

"Are they threatening you?" Jake asked. His heart was pounding and his stomach was in knots. The pizza he'd eaten only moments ago churned inside him.

"It's not your problem," Jennifer said defiantly. "I can deal with it."

"Mom, tell us!" Jake wouldn't take no for an answer.

There was a long pause before she spoke again. "These men started coming around as soon as I was out of the hospital. A guy named Valenti does most of the talking. He says Bull has their money, they want it back, and I have until Christmas to give it to them."

Jake and Taylor looked at each other. *Valenti.* Jake wondered if that was the man in the woods with Bull that night. Valenti must be the boss.

There was only one way out of this, he realized, but it would mean the end of everything. Bull's death would come out. Their dad might go to jail. But their mom would be safe.

"Mom, we've got to go to the cops."

"No!" Jennifer said instantly.

"But Valenti . . . he'll come for you . . ."

"Jake, I haven't finished. Valenti says he knows where Bull went. He says Bull took off after you boys. Valenti has been here. He took that school photo of the two of you. The one I kept on the bookcase. He knows what you look like."

"Oh no." Jake pressed his knuckles into his forehead and willed himself to keep it together.

"And I can't go to the police. Valenti said they'd find out if I did, and one of his men would kill me."

Taylor spoke into the phone. "Mom, remember Officer Grasso? Find him; he's a nice guy and can help."

Jake nodded in agreement. "And we'll get back there as soon as we can."

"No!" Jennifer exclaimed. "You boys stay *away*. Valenti's men are watching the house. I know they are!"

For a horrible moment Jake couldn't tell if his mom had gone crazy. What she'd just said suddenly sounded totally paranoid.

When Jennifer spoke again, however, she sounded perfectly sane. "The only thing that's kept me going this past week is knowing you boys are safe, and I want to keep it that way. Jake, promise me you'll stay with your father!"

Just then the band kids started streaming out of the pizza place toward the two motor coaches.

"Mom, we've got to go," said Jake. "We'll call you back as soon as we can."

"Go find Officer Grasso," Taylor shouted into the phone.

"JAKE! PROMISE ME! I WANT YOU TO—"

"I love you, Mom." Jake closed his eyes and ended the call, cutting his mom off midsentence.

The twins and Tess hurried up to them. "Did you get through?" Marty asked.

Jake's mouth was dry. "Yeah."

He tried to hand the phone back, but Marty shook his head. "No, you hang on to it for now, buddy. I'll say I lost it. Just mail it back to me when you get home. My address is in the contacts."

"Oh, man. Thanks. We owe you big-time." Jake switched the phone off to save on battery power and tucked it safely away.

"What are you going to do now?" Max asked.

"We've got to get back to Pittsburgh as fast as possible," said Jake.

"But how?" Tess asked.

"We need to catch a train," said Taylor. "Or a plane! We've got enough money for tickets, right, Jake?"

Jake gritted his teeth. "We need that money for *something else,* Taylor, or have you forgotten?"

The thought of giving Bull's money to Valenti made Jake feel sick to his stomach. Especially as they'd spent some of it.

"So, what do we do?" Taylor looked as if he were ready to collapse with exhaustion and despair.

Max and Marty grinned at each other, and at the brothers.

"What?" Jake asked. "What are you smiling about?"

Marty said, "We've got an idea."

16

"You can ride to Chicago with us!" Max said.

"What?"

"There's at least four or five empty seats," Marty explained. "And you can get halfway to Pennsylvania."

"People are going to notice," Jake objected. "And Ratzlaf won't get fooled twice. She'll bust us right away."

"Mrs. Ratzlaf rides in the other bus," said Tess, looking smug. "And the back-up bus driver will be asleep."

"Jake, listen," said Marty. "We're an all-district band. That means we come from schools all over the place. Marty, Tess, and I only know a few other kids from our school. Plus, we've only played together a few times, so most of these kids still don't know who's who."

"But what about Cody?" Taylor asked.

They all looked at Cody, wagging his tail, staring up at them.

"Does he bark a lot?" asked Tess.

"Not usually."

"Perfect," said Max. "We'll sneak you into the back row of the coach."

Jake looked at Taylor. "What do you think?"

Taylor didn't hesitate. "Let's go for it. What's the worst that can happen?"

Jake could think of half a dozen things, but agreed. "Okay. If it works, it'll save us a lot of time. We just need to get past the bus driver."

Max winked. "Leave that to us."

The driver stood next to the coach door, counting heads as students piled up the stairs. While Jake and Taylor hung back, Marty and Max took their large backpacks and snowshoes from them and carried them up to the driver. "Can we put these back in the luggage compartment?" Marty asked.

The driver scowled at the snowshoes. "What are those things? I don't remember seeing them before."

"They're snowshoes," Max explained. "We bought them as souvenirs."

The driver shook his head. "You kids. And now I lost my count."

While the driver walked down the side of the bus to open the lower baggage compartment, Tess hissed, "Now's our chance. Go!"

With Cody tucked snugly inside Taylor's parka, Tess led the boys onto the coach, and they quickly made their way to the back row of seats. A few students were already sitting there, but Tess smiled sweetly and asked them to move.

Jake and Taylor scooted into one side of the large backseat, and Tess sat next to them, blocking the driver's view of the boys. Moments later Max and Marty climbed up into the bus, each carrying a blanket and a pillow, grinning broadly. They grabbed their daypacks from where they'd been sitting before and made their way to the back of the bus.

"Chicago, here we come!" Max whispered, plonking down onto the other side of the bench seat.

Jake grinned. "Thanks, guys."

"Yeah," said Taylor. "That was pretty cool."

"We're not home free yet. Stay down," Tess warned as the bus driver climbed back onto the coach.

"Under the blankets, quick!" said Marty.

They hastily covered up Jake's and Taylor's hunched figures with the blankets, and Tess leaned on top of them to make it look like she'd just made a comfortable bed for herself. As the rest of the kids on the bus chatted noisily, the driver slowly shuffled down the bus aisle redoing his head count to make sure everyone was on board. He paused briefly, looking at Tess, Max, and Marty, but his numbers evidently tallied.

He spun around and walked back to the driver's seat.

After fastening himself in, he turned the ignition key, and the bus's giant engine roared to life.

So far, so good, thought Jake.

The pair of coaches drove two hours to Casper, where they picked up Interstate 25 heading east. Tess and Marty pulled out their tablets and tracked their progress using Google Maps. Jake and Taylor played with some game apps, which helped pass the time. Occasionally the kids glanced out the window to look at the snow-covered landscape. Twice they spotted groups of pronghorn antelope nibbling at the sagebrush along the interstate, and near Douglas they saw a billboard advertising the WORLD'S LARGEST JACKALOPE.

"Hey, look," Taylor said as the coach whizzed by without stopping. "How cool would it be to see a real-life jackalope?"

Jake elbowed him in the ribs. "You do know those things are made up, right? A rabbit with horns?"

"Duh. I still want to see it, though."

As they drove, Cody quickly became a secret celebrity for the kids in the back of the coach. A dozen kids scrounged through their daypacks to find him leftover sandwiches and other treats, and took turns petting and playing with the terrier.

As the miles rolled by, Jake pulled out Marty's phone and thought about calling their mom again. She'd told them not to come back to Pittsburgh, but Chicago wasn't Pittsburgh, was it? And they could hardly turn around and go back to Abe now.

He made up his mind and keyed in the numbers.

Click.

"Hi, this is Jennifer Wilder. . . ."

Jake waited for the beep.

"Mom?" he whispered. "Are you there? Mom, pick up."

There was no answer. Jake told himself not to panic. There were plenty of good reasons why his mom might not be answering. Maybe she was out at the supermarket.

"We're on a bus headed to Chicago," he said, glancing at Taylor's sleeping form humped over on the seat next to him. "We get in to Union Middle School at around noon tomorrow, okay? You could meet us there, if you want . . ."

Jake fought the growing suspicion that something was badly wrong. He gabbled out the number of Marty's phone, told his mom he loved her, and hung up.

Afterward he lay back and closed his eyes, savoring the comfort of the bus and the gentle hum of the engine. *I wish Dad were here,* he thought uneasily. *Dad would know what to do.*

Despite his anxiety, Jake slowly surrendered to the night and let his mind drift as the bus rolled through the gathering darkness.

With a jerk, Jake woke to the sight of cloudy skies reaching all the way to the horizon, and Taylor jabbing him in the side.

"Ow! Quit it!" he complained, pushing Taylor away from him.

"Time to get up, Bro. Look where we are."

Jake had slept the whole night as the coach had made its way across the country. Through the coach's smudged window, Jake could see the odd snowflake begin to fall as they passed the sign for Chicago, Illinois.

"We're nearly there!" Taylor said.

Jake groaned, still in a haze of sleep.

"Where are you guys going to stay?" Tess asked, leaning over the aisle between the seats. "We're nearly there."

"Nowhere," said Jake. "We have to keep moving." He said nothing about their mom maybe meeting them at the school. He wasn't even sure she'd gotten the message.

"Well, listen," Max interrupted, "we live pretty close by. Maybe you could come stay with us?"

"Thanks, but we can't stop."

As the coach pulled into the school parking lot and unloaded the passengers, the band members did their best to bunch up around Jake, Taylor, and Cody, hiding them from view. By the time they walked down the bus steps, all the bags and instruments were already stacked up in the parking lot next to the coaches. Taylor and Jake grabbed their backpacks and snowshoes, and turned to say quick good-byes to Marty, Max, and Tess.

"Thanks for your help," Jake said.

"No problem," Max replied.

"Yeah, it made the trip a lot more exciting," Marty said.

Tess smiled sadly. "Good luck, guys. If things don't work out in Pittsburgh, maybe you can move to Chicago?"

Taylor laughed. "We'll keep it in—"

"Hey!" a voice suddenly yelled. "Stop right there. Police!"

They all turned to see two men striding toward them, wearing long coats and dark glasses despite the overcast weather. One had dark hair and stubble, the other straw-colored hair that stuck out like a haystack. Jake caught sight of what might have been a gun under the unshaven man's coat.

"It's the cops!" Max gasped.

"How did they know?" asked Marty.

"Jake and Taylor Wilder? You need to come with us," called the policeman with dark hair as they approached.

Before anyone could react, Mrs. Ratzlaf came barreling over. "You two! I knew you were trouble. Don't move!"

Taylor gripped Jake's arm in panic. "Jake, what do we do?"

Jake's mind raced, even as his body stood frozen in stark terror. *Now it'll all come out. Bull's death . . . the money . . . Dad . . .*

He thought about running. Maybe they would make it halfway across the parking lot, but not much further. The cops had nearly reached them now. Even if Jake and Taylor managed to outrun them, the police would call for backup.

"Come on, Jake!" Taylor wailed. "Quick—we need to run!"

Jake put his arm around his brother and hugged Cody tight with the other arm. "No," he said in a hollow voice. "No more running."

17

Mrs. Ratzlaf's heavy hand clamped down on Jake's shoulder. "I knew these two weren't who they said they were," she announced to the approaching men. "Max and Marty, you have not heard the last of this! I'll be speaking to your parents!"

"I'm sorry," Jake told the boys. "Really."

Max shrugged, looking down at the ground. "I'm not. It was fun."

The stubbly man gave Mrs. Ratzlaf a tight-lipped smile. He pulled a badge out of his coat, flashed it quickly, and tucked it away again. "Detective Lorenzo, ma'am. This is my partner, Detective Blake."

Blake nodded. Jake noticed he was chewing something. Gum, or tobacco? Either way, it made Jake a little queasy to watch.

"These two boys—" Mrs. Ratzlaf began, but Detective Lorenzo hushed her. "We'll deal with them, ma'am. I'm sure you're very busy."

Mrs. Ratzlaf narrowed her eyes. "They lied to me! Don't I even get to know who they are?"

Lorenzo and Blake looked at one another.

"Well, I dunno who they claimed to be, but their names are Jake and Taylor Wilder," Lorenzo said. "They're runaways. There's been some trouble at home, but everything's okay now."

"Yeah, everything's just peachy," Blake chimed in, and grinned. Lorenzo gave him an irritated look. Blake shrugged and shut up.

"What do you mean, trouble?" Mrs. Ratzlaf demanded. She still had her hand on Jake's shoulder.

"Well, uh . . ." Lorenzo shuffled uneasily. "It seems their mom got mixed up with some nasty people. Criminals, you know? And these boys thought she was in danger, so they came all the way back from, uh, wherever they were. To help."

"But it's okay now," Blake said, cracking his knuckles. "Boys, your mom got your message, and she's come all the way to Chicago to meet you."

"She has?" Taylor burst out. "Jake, did you hear? Mom's okay!"

The two cops beamed.

Jake didn't even crack a smile. Something wasn't right.

"So, if you two boys would just come with us," Lorenzo said, holding out his hand, "we'll take you straight to your mom. Won't that be great?"

Mrs. Ratzlaf relaxed her grip on Jake.

"You should have told me something was wrong," she told him. There was real concern in her voice. "I could have helped you."

Jake hung his head. He couldn't think of what to say, so he said nothing at all. Grudgingly he followed Lorenzo and Blake through the parking lot, Mrs. Ratzlaf's eyes boring into the back of his head the whole way.

Taylor couldn't stop grinning. "Mom's in Chicago, Jake! We're finally going to see her again!"

"Yeah," said Jake.

"How did she know where we'd be?"

"I called her while you were asleep," Jake said. "Left a message on the answering machine. I wasn't sure she'd got it. . . ." His voice trailed off.

As they walked through the parking lot, shepherded by the two men, Jake's thoughts swirled in his mind. A troubling suspicion had started to form. Was he just being paranoid?

If Mom is really here in Chicago, why didn't she come to meet us herself?

They reached a shiny black car with tinted windows. Blake spat out the gum he'd been chewing and opened the door for them. "Get in, kiddos."

Cody wriggled and barked in Taylor's arms. "Easy, boy!" Taylor laughed, petting him.

Lorenzo climbed in and slammed the door. "Keep that mutt under control, okay?" he snapped. "I don't want to have to clean up no mess, you understand?"

"Oh . . . okay," said Taylor. "He'll be fine."

"Give the kid a break, would ya?" Blake said, giving Lorenzo a warning glance. "He's been through a lot!"

Lorenzo grunted and started the engine.

Jake sat in the back with his pack across his legs. His heart was pounding now. He was sure they were in more danger than they'd been since Bull was alive. His mind raced.

Something's not right. Mom didn't want to go to the police even to speak to Officer Grasso.

What was going on? *Was that even a real badge Lorenzo flashed?*

He licked his lips and tried to act normal. "So, where are your lights?" he asked, trying to keep his voice steady.

"Huh?" said Lorenzo.

"Your roof lights. The ones that flash."

There was a long, long pause. Cody whined. Lorenzo pulled out into traffic. Eventually he said, "Er . . . they're in the trunk."

"Yeah," Blake added. "We're undercover cops, so we've got those stick-on magnetic lights." He leaned back, satisfied with his answer.

Jake wasn't satisfied at all. What kind of cops didn't

have their lights ready to go? And why would they go undercover to pick up two kids?

The fear that had been growing now suddenly exploded into full-blown terror. Jake was certain that these two men weren't cops at all.

Taylor was talking to Cody in a low whisper, trying to calm him down. Jake's mind whirred as loud as the car's engine as he tried to piece everything together.

Who could have known we'd be arriving in Chicago on that bus? he asked himself. When he'd phoned home yesterday, nobody had answered. So he'd left a message. A message that anyone could have listened to.

In a flash he knew.

Valenti and his men were in the house yesterday! He must have been there and heard me leave my message. Then he called up two thugs in Chicago and gave them our names and our descriptions. And enough information to make their story convincing.

Jake looked out the window. They were in slow-moving traffic, heading over a bridge. And it wasn't the police driving them but criminals.

His mind went into overdrive. He thought about flinging the door open and running, but Taylor was a problem. He'd totally bought these guys' story.

Jake dug his water bottle out of his pack and took a swig. His hands were shaking. *I need to warn him.*

Blake twisted round in his seat, giving Jake a fake smile.

"So, buddy. You got any special souvenirs in that pack of yours?"

The money. He knows we've got Bull's money.

It took all of Jake's effort to keep his voice steady. He replied, "Just a half ton of deer jerky. You want to try some?"

"No thanks, I'll pass."

Lorenzo seemed to have an idea. "Hey, you kids must be hungry if all you've had to eat is crap like that. I'm going to take us to a diner, okay?"

"But what about our mom?" Taylor protested.

"Your mom's fine, kid, I told ya. We'll go see her straight after we've had something to eat. I promise."

They were heading out of central Chicago now. The buildings were looking more and more run-down.

Wherever these two are taking us, Jake thought, *it won't be a diner.*

He tried to guess what would happen next. Valenti's men might hold them hostage and use them to force their mom to do whatever he wanted. Or they might go through their bags and find the money. . . . Would that be enough to keep their mom safe anymore? She knew too much now. They all did.

Jake made up his mind. They had to escape. But first he had to warn Taylor.

Suddenly he had an idea.

Blake looked back suspiciously. "What you got there, kid?"

"Just my journal," Jake said innocently, pulling the notebook out of his pack and pretending to flip through the pages.

Blake turned back toward the road. Jake desperately flicked through the pages until he found what he was looking for. After the coyotes had attacked him, he'd drawn a sketch of them, prowling and mean-eyed. He showed it to Taylor.

"Hey, remember these guys?"

Taylor chuckled. "Of course I do."

Jake pointed to the words he'd written under the picture. *I didn't see them coming until it was too late. I should have known I was in danger.* He nodded slightly toward the criminals in the front seat and fixed Taylor with an intent stare, until a flicker of understanding crossed his brother's face.

"Do they remind you of anyone?" Jake said.

"Oh yeah." Taylor looked up at Blake and Lorenzo. "I know what you mean. You were lucky to get away, huh?" He gave Jake a quick nudge in the ribs.

"Uh-huh," Jake murmured. "Would you know what to do, if we got into another *jam* like that one?"

"Stick together, and get the heck out of there," said Taylor quietly.

"Hey, what are you two squawking about? Lemme look at that thing," Blake demanded, suddenly curious.

Jake reluctantly passed him the notebook. Blake riffled idly through the pages, as if he were just passing time.

But Jake could tell he was looking for a clue to where the money was.

Jake held his breath. He hadn't written anything about Bull or the money in there, so he knew Blake was wasting his time. It was just a record of their wilderness adventures, and the survival lessons they'd learned. But he still didn't want Blake's dirty fingers pawing at it.

Eventually Blake tossed it back to them, disappointed. "Not bad. You can draw, kid."

"Thanks." Jake tucked the notebook away, praying Blake hadn't smelled a rat. He knew they were running out of chances.

A few blocks further on, Jake finally saw his opportunity. Lorenzo swore under his breath and stopped the car.

A traffic light up ahead had just turned red, and traffic had slowed to a crawl. There were cars blocking the road ahead of them, behind, and in the other lane.

Now or never.

As the car began to move forward again, he wrenched at the door handle and shoved the door open. "Taylor, *go!*" Jake yelled. He grabbed his pack and scrambled out of the car onto the sidewalk and ran.

Behind him, Taylor did the same, still holding Cody in his arms. Lorenzo started to yell, and Blake threw open the passenger door. The traffic ahead of the car was moving now, but their car wasn't. Angry horns started to honk.

Jake glanced back. Taylor, to Jake's horror, was struggling

with his pack. Cody fell from his arms and came bounding after Jake.

"Leave it!" he hollered. "Run, Taylor. Just run!"

Taylor's face screwed up with effort as he sprinted after Jake. The abandoned pack sagged half out of the car.

Lorenzo gunned the engine and drove the car off the road and onto the sidewalk, out of the flow of traffic. Pedestrians jumped out of his way, shouting in alarm.

"Hold it right there!" Blake screamed. He had something in his hands . . . something black, metallic, and lethal. "FREEZE!"

18

The two boys ran down the sidewalk without looking back. Any second now Jake expected to hear the sharp bang of Blake's gun and for the world to go dark. Death had never seemed so close, not even in the wild. He had to find cover.

To his left he spotted an alley between two buildings. Urging Taylor to follow, he turned and ran down it. Dumpsters half-blocked his path, and trash crunched underfoot, but he ran on, gasping, with Cody and Taylor right behind him.

Yells and screams from the street behind told him Blake and Lorenzo were chasing them.

The alley opened up into a busy street, with cars rushing past in both directions. Jake knew he had to put more distance between himself and the men.

"Keep going!" he yelled to Taylor. "Cross the road!"

The second there was a lull in the traffic, Jake ran.

A horn blared.

From behind came a sickening *thump*, then a shrill yelp of pain.

Jake knew what had happened without having to turn round.

Taylor cried out in despair: "*Cody!*"

The little dog lay, his legs twitching, in the road. The car that had hit him had come to a stop a few yards ahead. There was blood on Cody's muzzle.

"Cody?" moaned Jake. "*No!*"

Jake dashed back into the road and gathered Cody up into his arms. The dog was shivering, forcing a whine out with every breath.

"You're going to be fine, little guy," he said, although he was far from sure that was true.

"Is he dead?" yelled Taylor.

"He's breathing. But he's hurt pretty bad."

The two boys ran the rest of the way across the street and looked back at the alley they'd come from. Blake came staggering out and looked left and right, hunting for them.

"Go!" Jake urged. They ran, dodging back and forth to avoid the people coming the other way. Jake's pack jolted and whacked against his back, and the straps dug into his shoulder. Cody felt heavy in his arms, like the limp rabbit he'd once carried back to his dad's cabin. There was a reason why people used the words "dead weight."

Stop it, he told himself. *No more death.*

"Jake," Taylor gasped, "where are we going?"

"I don't know!" Jake yelled. "Just run!"

Jake had no idea where in Chicago they were. It looked pretty built-up, so they were still within the city limits, but there were discount stores among the shops, and some vacant lots with peeling handbills plastered across the boards. In an area like this, Jake thought, you could easily take a wrong turn and end up somewhere shady. If someone ripped his pack away from him, they'd get Bull's money, and the boys' last hope of saving their mom would be gone.

His chest was aching with the effort of running. He couldn't tell if Cody was still breathing or not.

Got to go to ground, he thought. That was what hunted animals did. Before they collapsed from exhaustion, they bolted for a safe haven.

None of the shops looked like good places to hide. They might be able to push into a fast-food place and hide in the bathroom, but if Blake saw them go in, he'd just flash his fake badge to the management, then drag them out. They could run down another alley and try to hide in a Dumpster. It would stink, but they might be safe. Or they might be trapped like cornered rats.

Then Jake saw it, parked down a side street—their

hiding place. It was a custom pickup truck, shiny black with flames and skulls painted down the side. There was a tarpaulin over the cargo bed, with one corner loose.

"Taylor, c'mon!" He put on a burst of speed, caught the edge of the cargo bed one-handed, and scrambled up. Cody jerked in his arms, as if he were coughing out the last of his life. Jake noticed a wet blood spot on his shirt but tried not to think about it and instead held out a hand to help Taylor up.

A last glance over the side of the cargo bed showed no sign of Blake. The two brothers hunkered down in the dark space. Jake tugged the tarpaulin over their heads.

"Now what?" whispered Taylor.

"We just have to wait."

"But Cody . . . he might—"

"I know. But we can't go out there until it's safe!"

Jake heard his brother sniff back tears in the dark. Jake pretended he hadn't heard anything. He just put his arm around Taylor and hugged him close.

The weird part was how familiar it all felt. Only a few days before, they'd been huddled together in a snow house, in a cramped little space like this, unable to leave until it was safe, with the cries of wild animals on the wind outside. Now they were hiding in a stranger's truck on a back street of some unfamiliar city with criminals hunting them.

Jake waited for as long as he dared. Cody was still

shivering, and his breath came in shuddering gasps. Taylor tried to pet him and tell him it was going to be okay, but the dog yelped in pain the moment he was touched.

From outside came the sounds of passing traffic and the voices of people coming and going in the street, but though Jake braced himself for angry shouts, none came. A police siren wailed, briefly, in the distance. He wondered if someone had seen Blake waving the pistol around and had called 911. There was no way to know.

"Okay," he said eventually. "Let's move."

Taylor held on to Cody as Jake moved the tarpaulin back out of the way. They had begun to climb down, when Taylor gasped.

"Jake, look in the cab!"

"Huh?"

"Snake!"

"You're hallucinating, Taylor. You need to rest, get something to eat—"

Taylor pointed. "Look!"

A flat, scaly head reared up inside the truck cab, looking at them through the window glass. Jake stared at the long, sinuous body that was twined around the steering wheel and vanished into the foot well.

"I don't believe it," he breathed.

Jake had seen snakes before, but only in the wild, and never anything to compare with this. The reptile had to be six feet long, easy, from snout to tail. It slid along the back of the truck seats as if it owned them, watching Jake and Taylor with eyes like polished jet.

"What is it?" Taylor said. "An anaconda?"

A laugh came from the sidewalk. "No, Draco's a rock python. He's better than a vehicle alarm, huh?"

Jake gave a yell of surprise and half-jumped, half-fell from the back of the truck. The guy who'd spoken could only be the truck's owner, by the look of him—a tall, gaunt man with spiked-up hair, torn jeans, and a long leather coat, all as black as his truck. Jake saw complicated tattoos on the backs of his hands.

Behind him, walking up fast, was a girl with shocking pink hair shaved on the sides, and a T-shirt with a skeleton rib cage pattern. She folded her arms and glared at the boys with eyes that burned like lasers.

"We're sorry!" Jake burst out. "We needed a place to hide!"

"What'd you steal?" the man said calmly.

For a panicked moment Jake thought he must somehow know about Bull's money. Then he realized that wasn't possible. The man must have thought they were shoplifters. *We look like a couple of delinquents,* Jake thought.

"We didn't steal anything," Taylor said, and the desperation in his voice made the strange-looking couple stop in their tracks. "This guy was chasing us, and Cody—he's our dog—he got hit by a car!" Taylor held Cody's limp body out to them.

That changed everything. The girl strode up to Taylor. "Let me see."

Cody leaned up and, weakly, licked her cheek.

"I'm Jola," she said, "and this is Danny. You'd better bring Cody inside."

"Inside" turned out to be the apartment above a tattoo studio, reached via a graffiti-scrawled stairwell. Jake held tightly to his pack as they walked. These two might seem friendly, but he knew things could change in an instant.

"Would you cancel the last booking, hon?" Jola asked Danny as she unlocked the door. "I think my hands are going to be full for a while."

"No problem." In answer to the boys' questioning looks, Danny explained: "Our studio's downstairs. We're tattoo artists."

Jola showed them into the apartment. Jake looked around in amazement at the objects inside—amazing sculptures made from twisted metal and salvaged junk. Something like a bear loomed beside the door, with hubcap eyes and claws made from recycled tableware. A mantis, looking like it was welded together from motorcycle parts, stood guard at the end of the corridor. And inside the living room, beside the couch, sat the sculpture Jake instantly chose as his favorite, a wolf made from weathered iron and steel.

"Do you make all these?" he asked Jola.

She nodded. "I love animals. I trained to be a vet, but I

guess I'm an artist at heart. Now, Cody, let's take a look at you."

She gently laid Cody down on the couch. Jake and Taylor watched as she carefully felt his limbs, checked how his eyes reacted to light, and listened to the sound of his breathing.

Cody didn't even yelp anymore. He was completely out cold.

"Will he be okay?" Taylor whispered.

Without looking up Jola said, "Why don't you and your brother help yourselves to a drink? There's sodas in the fridge."

Jake understood. "Come on. Let's let her take care of him."

Danny came and joined them at the kitchen table, under a dangling giant hornet made from chrome and repurposed computer components. "What do you think?" he asked, jerking a thumb at it.

"The sculptures are amazing," said Jake.

"You can find a lot of good stuff in the city, if you know how to look," Danny said. "It's a sin what some people throw away. Such a waste."

That sounds familiar, Jake thought. Despite being in the city, Danny and Jola weren't so very different from them. They were using survival skills to get by too.

"We made these," he told Danny, pointing out the

fringed leather jackets he and Taylor wore. "Tanned the hides ourselves."

"Seriously?" Danny whistled. "Impressive."

"Dad always says we have to use the whole deer," Jake said. "Nothing gets wasted."

"I see where you're coming from," Danny said with a slow nod. "The city's like a wild place too, when you live like we do. You have to know its ways. What's safe to do and what's not."

"Dad hates cities," Taylor put in. "He says they're poison."

"Well, a lot depends on your point of view," Danny said, grinning. "I couldn't live a nine-to-five life, wearing a suit and tie. That'd kill me. But here it's different. 'Welcome to the jungle. We've got fun and games.'" He twiddled on an imaginary guitar, and the boys laughed.

The laughter died as Jola appeared in the doorway. Her fingers were bloody.

Taylor leaped up from his seat. "Is he . . ."

Jola smiled.

"Good news, boys. Cody is going to be fine." She put a tiny ivory-colored object down on the table. "He lost a tooth, and his hind leg's sprained, but he's a tough little cookie. He'll pull through."

Taylor whooped out loud. Jake leaned back in his chair, sagging with relief. *Thank God.*

"But," Jola said, "and it is a big 'but' . . ." She went to wash her hands in the sink while she talked. "He needs to rest up and get better. That means he can't run around after you. He needs to travel in a pet carrier or on a car seat."

Jake and Taylor exchanged horrified glances. "But we need to get to Pittsburgh!" Taylor said.

"Pittsburgh?" Danny echoed. "I thought you guys were from round here."

"Got someone to drive you?" Jola asked.

"No," admitted Jake. "We were going to get the train."

Jola gripped the edge of the sink and let out a long sigh. "Okay, let me give it to you straight. If you try to take that dog with you all the way to Pittsburgh, he might not heal up properly. Sorry, but those are the facts."

"But what else can we do? We can't leave him here!" cried Taylor.

"I can't believe I'm saying this, but . . . yes, you can."

"You'd do that?" Jake asked, stunned.

"Sure. I won't turn away an animal in need. I'll look after him until he's better, if you need me to, and you can pick him up in a week or so. I like the little guy. He's a fighter." She splashed cold water onto her face and toweled off. "Or you can take him with you and run the risk of his leg never healing right."

"That's a really tough decision," Jake said, frowning.

"Yeah. But, it has to be your decision. Not ours."

Jake turned his face away. He already knew what he had to do.

19

Danny drove like he was playing a video game. Jake and Taylor were flung this way and that as Danny threw the truck around tight bends, racing to reach Union Station in time to catch their train. Fortunately, Jola had taken Draco the python out before they'd climbed in.

"Aww, come on, Grandpa, get out of the way!" Danny yelled at a slow-moving driver in front of him. "We're on a mercy mission here!"

Jake glanced at Taylor, hoping to see him grinning in excitement. But the boy just sat, unsmiling, letting the motion of the truck jostle him around. It was as if something inside him had broken.

"Hey, champ," Jake said. "It's going to be okay."

"No, it's not," Taylor said.

"You heard Jola. Cody will be fine. He just needs to rest up."

"We left him behind," whispered Taylor. "It was my fault. I should have been holding him . . ."

Jake understood now. No wonder Taylor had been so quiet since they'd left Danny and Jola's apartment. It wasn't just the sorrow of abandoning Cody. It was guilt.

"Don't talk like that. You aren't to blame. You know who is?"

Taylor shook his head and sniffed.

"Valenti. He sent those two creeps after us. He threatened Mom, and it's his fault Cody nearly got killed. We're going to make him pay."

They were both flung forward, then back, as Danny brought the truck to a screeching halt outside Union Station. Jake smelled the acrid tang of burning rubber.

"Got you here in one piece!" Danny yelled triumphantly.

"Mostly," Jake said, rubbing his neck.

"Okay, guys. Train to Pittsburgh leaves in ten minutes. Look, here's our card—it's got everything on it, phone, address . . ."

"Thanks—" Jake began.

"No time for long good-byes," Danny cut in. "You guys gotta go, go, go!"

Jake and Taylor piled out of the truck, waved to Danny, and ran into the station. Jake was glad he'd counted out the money for their tickets in advance. Pulling out the entire wad of money would have attracted a lot of attention, especially looking as wild as they did.

He bought the tickets from a surly attendant who didn't even look up. "You'll have to hurry," the man said, even as it took him forever to punch in the purchase on his screen. "You don't get no refund if you miss your train."

"I get it," Jake said, snatching up the tickets the man finally doled out.

Four minutes to go. They hurried through the crowds, hunting for their platform.

"There it is!" Taylor said, pointing toward a sign at the other end of the station.

The concourse was teeming with people studying the departures board, buying snacks at kiosks, and greeting friends. Jake and Taylor zigzagged through the crowd, skirting around weary travelers wheeling suitcases and pushing strollers.

"Excuse me," said Jake, navigating past a large family saying a tearful farewell to an elderly relative.

"Final boarding for the Capital Express, stopping in Cleveland, Pittsburgh, and Washington, DC," came an announcement over the loudspeaker.

"We're going to miss it!" cried Taylor as they sprinted toward their platform.

As they neared the platform, a small vehicle pulling a luggage cart piled high with suitcases barred the way. It had stalled in front of the platform entrance, completely blocking the passage. Jake looked frantically left and right, but there was no room to squeeze past. There was only one thing to do—

"Jump!" shouted Jake, leaping onto the cart and scrambling over the baggage. He didn't even look behind him to see if his brother had followed his lead.

"Hey, what do you think you kids are doing?" shouted the man driving the luggage cart.

"All aboard!" called the loudspeaker.

Jake ran to the train. His heart was pounding so hard, it felt like it would shatter his rib cage, but he didn't stop. He could hear Taylor panting and gasping as he ran behind him.

The last time they'd run to catch a train, it had been a freight train out of Pittsburgh; now it was one going in the opposite direction. Both times urgency had coursed through Jake's veins.

He sprinted up to the train, yanked open the carriage door, and climbed on board. Hauling Taylor up behind him, he panted with relief as the train guard blew his whistle and the train lurched forward.

"Phew!" gasped Taylor, clutching his side. "Pittsburgh, here we come!"

Later, after they'd found their compartment and stowed Jake's pack, the boys sat munching burgers they'd bought from the dining car. Jake tore off a piece of meat without thinking and felt a sudden pang of loss. He'd meant to feed it to Cody, but their little terrier wasn't there. Sharing food with the dog had become second nature to him.

"Man, I still can't believe we made it," Taylor said, chuckling. "That was a close call."

Jake shrugged. "We've made it this far. I wasn't going to let a stupid luggage cart get in the way of us getting on the train. Not after all we've been through."

"Yeah. Remember that time when Cody . . ."

Taylor's voice trailed off. He yawned.

Jake sighed, stood up, and folded the seat down to make a bed. "You can sleep if you want. We've got a long way left to go."

"What about you? Don't you need to sleep too?"

Jake looked out the window at the dark countryside, with the white moon high above. It was lighting their way home, to their mom, and to Valenti. He had to be ready to meet that threat.

"Not yet," he said. "I've got too much on my mind."

Later, Jake sat writing in his journal while the train rushed on toward Pittsburgh. Taylor lay curled up on his makeshift bed, snoring, a pillow in his arms the way he usually cuddled Cody.

When they got to Pittsburgh, they'd need a plan. They had to be ready to face Valenti and his men. Jake knew it wouldn't be easy, but he and Taylor were hunters. They knew how to track and trap prey in the woods. Now they just had to figure out how to do it in the city.

20

"Jake, wake up!"

Bright light was in Jake's eyes. He blinked and jerked upright. "Where are we?"

"Pittsburgh! We're home!"

Home. The word had an electric effect on Jake. Suddenly he was no longer tired. The train was slowing down, almost at its final destination.

"I woke up an hour ago," said Taylor, "but I let you sleep."

They packed Jake's bag one last time and hurried to the door. Passengers were already waiting to disembark.

When the train finally stopped and they could step out onto the platform, the strangeness of it all hit them. They were finally home, among old, familiar sights—but there was a strangeness about it. Somehow it felt smaller.

They took the bus back to their old neighborhood. Jake took out Marty's phone, thinking maybe he should call the house and let their mom know they were coming, but then he tucked it away again. Valenti might be there. Better not give him a warning.

Together Jake and Taylor walked back down the route they knew so well. Thick gray skies had settled overhead, and a bone-chilling wind whistled over brown lawns and down empty streets.

"Where is everyone?" Taylor asked as they passed the church and the houses of neighbors.

"School? Work? Staying warm indoors? They're not all outdoor types."

That reasoning, though, didn't keep the knot out of Jake's stomach as they turned onto their old street and caught sight of their house.

As they approached, Jake looked at it closely. Little had changed. White paint still peeled from the wooden siding, and a few more slats had fallen off the wooden fence, but it was basically the same old house they'd left five months before.

So why does it feel so different? Jake wondered.

"It doesn't look like anyone's home," Taylor said.

"Only one way to find out."

Slowly Jake walked up to the ragged screen door that Bull had torn off in a rage right before the boys had left home. Taylor hesitated at the foot of the steps, and Jake could tell that he, too, was afraid of what they might discover. But Taylor took a deep breath and climbed the stairs one at a time. He knocked.

Nothing happened.

"Try again," Jake said.

Taylor banged on the door more loudly this time, but again there was no response.

"I don't hear anyone moving inside," Taylor said. "Maybe she's out?"

Jake didn't think so. "Let's go round the back. Maybe we can—"

Taylor hopped back down the steps, and they began to walk toward the corner of the house. Suddenly, though, they heard the front door squeak open behind them.

"Jake! Taylor!"

The boys spun around to see Jennifer, standing in the front doorway.

Jake's heart almost leaped out of his chest. "Mom!"

Jake and Taylor scrambled back up the steps and launched themselves into their mom's waiting arms.

"I didn't think I'd ever see you again," Jennifer gasped, grabbing them both tight and wrapping them up in a huge bear hug.

Jake let the tears spring from his eyes. Suddenly he knew what had been missing from Pittsburgh.

They sat around the kitchen table, gazing at each other like two alien species. Jake took a sip of water to wet his dry mouth. Compared to the clean taste of ice melt, city water would take some getting used to.

Jen took a deep breath. "Where have you two *been*?"

The story came flooding out of the boys. They told their mom everything. How they'd run away, the people they'd met, the places they'd stayed. They told her about the trucker lady, and the snowboarders, and Abe's cabin, and about the months they'd spent learning how to live off the land.

She stared, and nodded, and listened.

"And what about Bull?" she interrupted while Jake was talking about the coyotes. "Did he hurt you? Have you seen him?"

Jake swallowed. "Mom . . ."

"I need to know! If Valenti can track down Bull, he might leave me alone!"

Panic bubbled up inside Jake. "We don't know where Bull is."

"Jake Wilder!" He could feel himself buckling under his mom's accusing glare. "I want the truth out of you. Has Bull threatened you? Has he hurt you?"

"Bull's *dead*!" Taylor yelled suddenly. He leaped up, and his chair fell backward with a clatter. "Don't you get it, Mom? He's dead and he's never coming back."

"What?" Jen gasped.

"He can't hurt you anymore. You never have to worry about him again. He's dead, and I'm not sorry!"

Jen became pale and very still. "What happened?"

"Dad didn't kill him," Jake said quickly. "They had a fight, but Bull died by accident. He fell into a river and got washed over the edge of a waterfall."

As he spoke the words, he felt as if gallons of pent-up poison were pouring out of his body. He laid his arms on the table and his head on top of them, drained. Finally he'd told his mom the truth.

Jen's lips trembled. "And did your father go to the police?"

"No," Jake croaked. "We never talked about it."

"Oh, my poor boys. How did you get tangled up in this?" A look of rage crossed her face. "I never wanted this!"

"We know, Mom," Jake said. "That's why we had to come back."

"We need to be a family again," Taylor said.

Jen clenched her fists. "I used to think we could have that with Bull, once your father left. I thought it would be good for you to have a man around. But I was wrong, wasn't I?"

Jake just lowered his eyes.

Jen held out her arms, and the two boys gathered with her into a close hug. It was over. All the guilt he'd carried, all the fear, washed away in that moment. He could face what still lay ahead without carrying those burdens anymore.

"Mom," said Taylor carefully, "why did Dad leave—"

Before Jen could say a word, the loud ring of the phone sounded from the hall.

"Uh-oh," she gasped, and put her hand to her mouth.

Jake grabbed her shoulders. "Don't answer it!"

"I have to!"

With the boys following, she ran to the hall and snatched up the phone. "Hello?"

Jake could hear a harsh voice snarling down the phone line. He knew it was Valenti even before his mom mouthed the name to him.

"I told you, I don't know where Bull is!" she said angrily. "He's gone. I don't know anything about any money!"

Valenti was shouting down the phone now. Jen held the receiver away from her ear and gritted her teeth.

Jake strode forward and snatched the phone out of her hand.

"Jake, give that back—" his mom began, but he was already across the room.

"Mr. Valenti," he said calmly. "This is Jake Wilder. Don't bother my mom again."

Valenti's laugh rang in his ears. "Hey, kid. Back from Chicago, huh? I heard you gave my guys there the slip."

"I can give you what you need," said Jake. "You want Bull. I'll bring him to you."

"You got him there? Sit tight. I'll be right over."

"He's not here," Jake said. "And you're not listening. I said I'll bring him to you." He closed his eyes; this next part was crucial. "There's a patch of scrubland not far from our house. Used to be a trailer park. You know it?"

A pause as Valenti spoke to his men. Then: "The jungle? Yeah. I know it."

"Noon, tomorrow. Be there. I'll make sure Bull's there." He hung up.

Jake turned to see his mom staring at him in fear and confusion. "Jake, what do you think you're doing?"

"It's okay, Mom," Jake said seriously. "Trust me. I just need to make one more phone call."

Jake remembered what Danny and Jola had said, that there are wild places in cities, too. . . .

The ring of disused trailers surrounding the clearing reminded Jake of a monument, a strange post-apocalyptic Stonehenge. Nearby, the woods waited, the perfect place to retreat to if it came to that. All sorts of trash lay piled up against the trailers: the remains of burned-out cars, old boxes and plastic bags, abandoned couches, and even a kid's plastic tricycle.

Jake sat waiting behind the largest trailer. It was two minutes to noon. Jake heard a car engine in the distance, growing nearer. Valenti was right on time.

He and Taylor had worked hard all morning to get ready. Now it was down to Jake. The trick was to not get cocky. He needed a hunter's patience.

Across the clearing a car pulled up. Two men stepped out from the front. Jake's chest tightened as he saw it was Blake and Lorenzo. A third figure emerged from the back, squinting in irritation at the bright light. That had to be Valenti himself, all six-foot of him.

Here we go, Jake thought. He pulled himself up a rusting ladder until he could perch on the trailer's roof and look down into the clearing.

Valenti stepped forward and arched his brow at the lanky, long-haired boy on the roof in front of him. "This what you wanted, kid? High noon, or whatever?"

"Something like that," Jake called. The three men looked up to where he stood.

Valenti chuckled. "You got guts, I'll give you that. I guess you're the man of the house now, huh?"

"I don't hide behind hired thugs, if that's what you mean," Jake said coolly.

Valenti's face darkened. "I want Bull, and I want my money. Hand 'em over. Or you'll wish you'd never crossed me."

"What's the hurry?" Jake said, sitting down cross-legged on the trailer roof. "The way I hear it, people cross you all the time. You're too chicken to do your own killing."

"You little brat," Valenti spat. "I don't need to get my hands dirty takin' out trash, you understand me? When I pay for some guy to get hit, that guy gets hit. And Bull screwed up!"

"Boss . . . ," Blake said cautiously.

"What?" Valenti yelled. "This kid's just a punk! He don't know who he's dealing with! You think I got to watch my mouth around him, huh?" He pulled a gun out of his coat and waved it at Jake. "Last chance. Show me where Bull is."

"In there," Jake said. He pointed to one of the old trailers.

Valenti nodded to Blake. "Check it out."

Blake pulled out his own pistol and hesitantly edged across the clearing. Fallen leaves rustled underfoot. He reached out and took hold of the trailer's door handle. He tugged.

"It's stuck," he complained. "Rusty."

"Pull harder!" Valenti ordered.

Blake gave the handle a vicious tug. The door flew open—and the loop of rope that had lain hidden under the leaves whipped tightly around Blake's leg. From his perch on top of the trailer, Jake could clearly see the tree branch he'd bent back to make the snare, and the rope that fed through a broken trailer window. As the trap fired, Blake was pulled off his feet. His gun flew up into the air, and his head cracked on the ground, knocking him out cold. Taylor's trap had worked.

One down, thought Jake, *two to go.*

"What the . . . ," Valenti yelled, backing away.

The trailer door slammed back. Officer Grasso stepped out, gun in hand. "Freeze, the pair of you. You're under arrest."

Valenti stood paralyzed for a moment. Jake knew what he must have been thinking. He'd boasted about paying to have people killed. He'd even talked about how Bull had "screwed up" a hit. And Officer Grasso had heard it all.

With a howl of frustration Valenti opened fire.

Officer Grasso ducked back inside the trailer. From somewhere close by came the whoop of a police siren. *Grasso's backup*, Jake thought. He lay down flat on the trailer roof, ducking the whirring bullets.

He heard Grasso return fire.

"I'm hit!" Lorenzo yelled.

Valenti cursed.

Jake heard feet running fast through dry leaves. He pressed down against the rusted metal. The backup would be here any second.

Suddenly Valenti came running right toward him—he was making a break for it.

But Jake was ready. As Valenti squeezed between two of the rusting trailers, Jake followed him above.

"There's no way out," Jake called.

"Oh yeah? We'll see about that," Valenti sneered. He raised his arm and fired up at Jake. Jake dodged just in time, pressing himself flat against the trailer roof. Then clambered to his feet and resumed the chase.

There was only one way to stop Valenti now.

21

With a howl of rage Jake jumped from the trailer roof. He crashed into Valenti, knocking him sprawling to the ground. The gun went off with a crack, reverberating in the air.

Jake tried to stand but couldn't. Searing pain shot up his left leg. *My ankle,* he realized painfully. It was clearly twisted.

Valenti scrambled to his feet. He loomed over Jake, readying his gun. Jake's boot had caught him in the face, and now blood streamed freely from the gangster's nose and over his bared teeth.

"Nowhere to run this time," he said. "Lights out."

Jake stared down the gun barrel.

Then a dark shape came striding out from the wreck of

a nearby trailer. A heavy fist shot out and whacked Valenti's head. His eyes rolled up and he collapsed, giving way from the knees up, like a building hit by a wrecking ball. He toppled over and lay still.

Jake blinked. It wasn't Officer Grasso. Instead a familiar, bearded face stared down at him.

"Dad?"

Jake felt strong arms lifting him up. The world swam in and out of focus. He lay draped across his dad's shoulder, smelling the familiar odor of leather and earth, the smell that meant he was safe.

Then he passed out.

When Jake woke up, he was back in his old bed, in his old house. He knew it hadn't been a dream. The pain in his ankle was proof enough of that. Something downstairs was cooking, and it smelled delicious.

He hobbled downstairs to find his mom and brother in the kitchen. "Jake, get back to bed!" his mom ordered him. "I was going to bring you up some lunch."

"Where's Dad?"

"He's at the police station," Taylor said.

"What's he telling them?"

"Everything. He's handed the money in too."

So, it's really over, thought Jake. *No more secrets.*

He settled painfully into a chair. "Did they get Valenti?"

"Yes, they did," Jennifer told him. "And the others.

Officer Grasso is a very happy man. He's been after that gang for a while, it turns out."

She set a plate of bacon and eggs down in front of Jake. Before he could take more than a few mouthfuls, the doorbell rang. Taylor bounded off to answer it.

Abe came into the kitchen, looking nervous. "Well, that's that." He tugged at the zipper on his parka. "Hey, Jake. Glad to see you're up."

Jake sat for a moment, savoring the sight of his mom and dad in the same room. It was like his two worlds were colliding.

"I can't believe you're both here," he said. "In the same room."

"Neither can I," said Jennifer, with a hard edge to her voice.

"It wasn't easy tracking you down," Abe said, half to the boys, half to Jennifer.

"Really? I would've thought it was easy," Jennifer flared. "The boys came home, and as for me, I didn't go anywhere in the first place."

Abe shifted awkwardly from one leg to the other—he didn't have an answer for that. The atmosphere was thick with regret.

Taylor jumped in. "How'd you find us?"

"I knew where you guys were going, but I was hoping I could catch up with you before you got here. So I went looking for you. I stopped at police stations. I showed your picture at every restaurant and gas station in Jackson, Riverton, and Lander. Finally, in Thermopolis, I ran into a girl Kim and her mom who said you'd stayed with them."

"You talked to Kim?" Taylor exclaimed.

"Yes," Abe continued. "She showed me the little carving of the grizzly bear you gave to her. She told me you'd headed into Thermopolis to try to catch a bus back to Pittsburgh. When I heard that, I headed straight back east."

"But how did you find us *here*?" Jake pressed.

"Well, I remembered you boys talking about an Officer Grasso, so I got in touch with him. He didn't want to tell me anything at first, but I managed to convince him that I was your dad and that I didn't work for that criminal—what was his name?"

"Valenti," Taylor said. "So that's when you came here?"

"Well, uh, not exactly," Abe said. "Once they realized who I was, and that I was involved with Bull's, um, demise, they interviewed me. They asked all about my life in Wyoming, and wanted to know all the details of Bull's death. They're going to want to take statements from you two, but they say it's unlikely I'll face prosecution."

"So you're all clear?" Jennifer asked flatly. "They're not going to press charges?"

"Knock on wood, it doesn't look like it." Abe tapped the back of a kitchen chair.

The four of them remained silent, none of them meeting

the others' gaze. Jake plucked up his courage and looked straight at his dad. "That still doesn't answer the question of *why* you're here."

"Ah, no, it doesn't." Abe cleared his throat. "I, uh . . ."

Jake, Taylor, and Jennifer watched as Abe struggled to find words to explain his sudden appearance. None of them stepped in to make it easier.

"Uh, the real reason I came—other than to make sure you boys were safe—was to, uh . . ."

"To what?" Taylor finally asked.

"Because I owe you all an apology. An apology for a lot of things," Abe said. "Back in Wyoming, I was too stubborn. I shouldn't have been so hard on you."

"That's an understatement," said Jake.

"I know. I had to have everything my way, and I'm sorry."

Abe looked Jennifer straight in the eyes. "Jennifer, I was wrong. I know that now. I was so invested in my big dream, I expected—no, I *needed*—everyone else to fall into line. Well, that's all over now. The big dream is officially dead."

Jennifer's face remained steely, but her eyes were wet and shining. "Thank heaven you get your brains from my side of the family, boys, because your father has nothing but cold oatmeal between his ears, and that's a fact."

"Jennifer, let me explain—"

"No, you let me explain," Jennifer started angrily. "Do

you think you can walk in here after seven years and for it all to be okay?"

Abe seemed taken aback.

"Do you know what I've had to put up with? I tried to do my best for the boys, but ended up with a criminal like Bull."

Jake and Taylor looked on awkwardly. Their mom crossed the room and looked into Abe's eyes.

"Jen—"

"No, it's my turn to talk," she insisted. "You still don't understand, do you? I married you *because* you were a dreamer. But it wasn't supposed to be just *your* dream; it was meant to be *ours*. We were meant to do it together—when we were ready."

"I-I thought you didn't want it anymore."

"I didn't want it on your terms," she finished, her anger lessening but her resolve firm.

Jake let their argument hang in the air for a minute. He hadn't been expecting this scene, and he didn't know what he should be doing. Except he knew he hadn't trekked half-way across the country, twice, to argue.

"The dream doesn't have to die," he whispered. "Not if we work on it together."

"That's a nice thought, Jake, but I don't think—" Abe began.

"Sounds like a good idea to me," Taylor chipped in.

"And at least we'll have tried," Jake said with a shrug.

Nobody said anything for a full minute. Abe looked nervously at Jennifer. "Or maybe I should just leave . . ."

"Again? I don't think so," Jennifer flared up once more. "Taylor . . . set another place for lunch, would you, honey?"

"Sure thing, Mom," Taylor said, and grinned.

Jennifer looked Abe up and down. "You'd better take off that coat, Abe Wilder. You aren't going anywhere."

EPILOGUE

Jake and Taylor hopped off the half-size rural school bus and waved good-bye to the driver. As usual, the brothers were the last students off the bus, since their stop was at the very end of the route home. It took them a full forty-five minutes to get to school and back, but neither of them minded. The bus allowed them to attend a real school again, something they'd missed during their months living alone with Abe in the mountains.

As the bus roared away, the boys heard a familiar bark and saw Cody racing down a mud-puddled dirt road toward them. Taylor squatted down to let the terrier crash into him.

"Hey! How's our boy?" Taylor shouted, scratching Cody behind the ears. "Did you chase lots of deer today?"

"Man, I hope not," said Jake. "With their new fawns

around, those white-tailed moms could kick field goals with him."

Taylor laughed and stood back up. "Cody's too smart for that."

"Aren't you forgetting a certain skunk he met a few weeks ago?"

"Well," Taylor said, "apart from that."

Lifting their daypacks up onto their shoulders, the boys started walking up the muddy road toward their house. Blue penstemon, lupine, and arrowleaf balsamroot bloomed all around them, and the songs of chickadees, nuthatches, bluebirds, and flickers filled the air. Jake sucked in the sweet, damp spring air, and said, "Man, I love it out here."

Taylor looked at him. "You don't ever miss Pittsburgh?"

"I miss some of the people. Officer Grasso and our old neighbors. What about you?"

"Yeah, I miss them. But, Jake, Wyoming is where we're supposed to be, don't you think?"

Jake nodded. "Yep."

Suddenly Taylor shouted, "Hey, look!"

Jake glanced up the road and spotted Abe and Jennifer walking toward them holding hands. The sight made him smile. When Abe had come east to find them, he and Jennifer had had to work hard to reestablish a relationship after so many years. There had been plenty of arguments—often involving Jake and Taylor, too. What was different now was that both of the boys' parents seemed determined to work through their problems. More important, for the first time in his life, Abe was learning to compromise.

And it's paying off, Jake thought, watching his parents approach, hand in hand. Jake had begun to feel like he was part of a real family again.

"What are you both doing home?" Taylor called to Abe and Jennifer. "Did Jackson close up early?"

Jennifer laughed and halted in front of the boys. "Early finish today!"

Jake smiled.

I haven't seen Mom look this happy in years.

Since leaving Pittsburgh, Jennifer's health had improved dramatically. Whether it was the clean mountain air or being a real family again, Jake didn't know, but for the first time in years his mother had plenty of energy. Recently she'd even started working again, finding a part-time job as a legal assistant in Jackson, where the boys went to school.

"What about you, Dad?" Taylor asked. "Did they close down Grand Teton National Park, too?"

Abe, still wearing his park ranger uniform, also chuckled. "Nope, but Skeet and I have to head out tomorrow for an overnight trip to track some wolverines. The District Ranger said we could take the afternoon off to get ready."

"So we thought we'd surprise you and walk home with you," Jennifer filled in.

Taylor and Jake grinned as they all continued up the road toward the park service house that had been provided for them. Unlike Abe's old cabin in the woods, this house had electricity and running water. Even though they had a stove indoors, Abe had built a fire pit outside, and in summer they cooked on it most days.

"So," said Jennifer, "since we're all home early, what should we do with the afternoon? We could go for a hike? I'm hearing a lot of new songbirds. Maybe you boys might get some new ones to add to your life lists?"

"Or," said Taylor, "we could play a game of horseshoes in the front. What do you think, Jake?"

Jake had been looking forward to lying in the backyard hammock and reading one of the new books he'd checked out from the library, but he nodded and said, "Horseshoes sounds good."

"How about a hike and then horseshoes?" Abe chimed in.

Jennifer elbowed him in the ribs. "Since when did you become so accommodating?"

Abe looked down at her and grinned. "Well," he admitted, "I've had three very good teachers the last few months. Although, I do have one suggestion."

"And what's that?" Jennifer asked.

"Well," Abe said, "how about you boys fill up those notebooks of yours, while you can still remember the details."

Jennifer nodded. "That's a *great* idea! After horseshoes we can take a hike, eat some dinner, and then spend the evening recording your adventures."

"Oh man," moaned Taylor. "I'm never going to fill up that journal you got me."

"You don't have to fill the whole thing," Abe told him.

"Just write what you remember," Jennifer chipped in.

"I doubt I'll even fill up half of the pages," Taylor said.

Abe patted him on the back and winked at Jake. "That's nothing to worry about, buddy."

"What if there are still a bunch of leftover pages in the back of the book?"

"Then," Jake said, "you'll have plenty of room to write about our other adventures."

Taylor looked at him curiously. "*What* other adventures?"

Jake punched him in the shoulder. "The adventures that are still to come."

WILDERNESS TIPS

Polaris, the North Star

Polaris is one of the brightest stars in the night sky and can be seen from across the northern hemisphere. You don't even need a telescope to find it. Just look at the Little Dipper constellation. Polaris sits right at the end of the "handle."

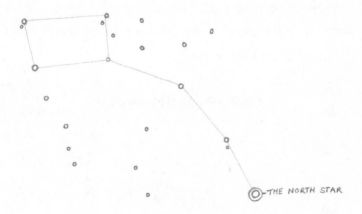

THE NORTH STAR

Polaris is called the North Star because it's so useful for navigation. Unlike other stars, the North Star hangs directly above the North Pole and never appears to move in the sky. If you can't find your way or don't have a compass, you can always find which way is north by looking up into the sky.

Arrowleaf Balsamroot

When boiled in water, arrowleaf balsamroot can help boost the immune system. Native Americans also used the roots and shoots for cooking, and even the young stems make for a quick, nutritious snack.

Deadly Parasol Mushroom

Some parasol mushrooms are edible, but get the wrong one, and it can prove deadly. NEVER EAT it if it has green gills or a green spore print. They are very poisonous and can even result in death. Always triple-check when dealing with the parasol.

Berry Cobbler in Dutch Oven

Ingredients:

4 cups of mixed berries (blueberries, raspberries, blackberries, strawberries)

juice from 1 lemon

¼ cup of water

2 cups of flour

1 tbsp. of baking powder

a pinch of salt

1 ½ cups of milk

1 stick of butter

1 tbsp. cinnamon

2/3 cup of sugar

Directions:

Wash and drain mixed berries.

In a large bowl mix the berries with sugar, lemon juice, and a splash of water.

In another bowl, mix flour, baking powder, and salt. Add milk and mix until batter is smooth.

Place the Dutch oven over the heat. Melt the butter.

Pour the batter over the melted butter, without stirring. Add spoonfuls of the berry mixture on top of the batter and sprinkle with cinnamon.

Put the lid on the oven and cook for 45–60 minutes, until the top is golden brown.

How to Build a Snow Cave

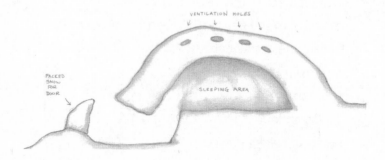

1. Find or build a mound of hardened, compact snow.
2. Take sticks and lay across the snow pile. These will be the rafters of the cave's ceiling.
3. Dig down into the side of the snow mound to create an entrance to the snow cave.

4. Then dig upward to create a sleeping area.
   The coldest air will fall down toward the door,
   creating a heat trap in the raised sleeping area.
5. Make sure to poke ventilation holes up through
   the snow roof.
6. Pack the entrance with snow, leaving a hole for
   ventilation.

Snowshoes

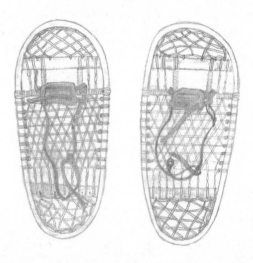

Snowshoes let people walk across deep snow without their
feet sinking right through it. The shoes work by distributing
weight evenly, so that you can move quickly across other-
wise impassable terrain. They've been in use for thousands
of years; it is believed that the very first snowshoes were
used in Central Asia in about 4000 BC!

There are hundreds of different ways to make snowshoes.

Here is one way to make a wooden snowshoe.

1. The wood is split by hand, to get the smoothest and straightest grain.
2. The long, thin strip of wood is steamed to make it flexible.
3. Once the wood is pliable, it is shaped into a teardrop shape (kind of like a big tennis racket) and left to dry in a kiln or a warm room.
4. Holes are drilled for the laces and the wooden slats that go across the middle.
5. The laces are tightly woven in an intricate pattern.
6. A binding is placed on top to hold the foot to the snowshoe.

Animal Tracks (Footprints)

White-Tailed Deer

Mule Deer

Rabbit

BRANDON WALLACE

Trekking solo across the most remote corners of Wyoming and Montana as a young man, Brandon learned the hard way how to survive in the harshest conditions nature could throw at him. Having spent the subsequent two decades as a trail leader, passing on his knowledge to a generation of budding adventurers, he turned his hand to fictionalizing his experiences, and *Wilder Boys* was born.

2198231998689